Ellen and the Three Predictions

Alayne Smith

Ellen and the Three Predictions

Internal photos of David Brinkley and Fidel Castro:
https://www.commons.wikimedia.org/

Internal photos of Jenny Lake in Wyoming courtesy of the US National Park Service

Saturn's Moon Press is an imprint of Cactus Moon Publications
For information address Cactus Moon Publications, LLC
1305 W. 7th Street, Tempe, AZ 85281
www.cactusmoonpublishing.com

First Edition

ISBN 978-0-9975363-7-9

To the future generations of broadcast Journalists.

Acknowledgments

With gratitude and respect to Father Bryan O. Walsh and James Baker whose humanitarian efforts brought so many children to safety during Operation Pedro Pan.

Dawn Richerson, an amazing editor, made *Ellen and the Three Predictions* so, so much better.

Thank you to Kolinda Scialabba, Coordinator of Broadcast Media at Gwinnett County Public Schools, for her expertise and encouragement during the entire writing process. She assured me that, if I was going to write, I had to let someone read my work.

Thank you to Mary Flynt, who provided me a window into Operation Pedro Pan.

I am thankful for my son Jeff's technical skills; he saved my neck on numerous occasions. Kudos to him for his amazing photographs in Ellen's Notebook.

My daughter-in-law, Katie Hart Smith, set my feet on the right path not once, but twice. She sets up a great website as well.

I so appreciate my husband, L.C., who read the first very rough draft and gave me an A+. I assure you it was an undeserved A+ at that point. He has supported me through the writing of *Ellen and the Three Predictions* as well as everything else I've tackled during my life. I am blessed to have him and our children—Jeff, Katie, Doug, and Christy—in my life.

Agent Johnnie Bernhard connected *Ellen and the Three Predictions* with Lily Woodmansee of Cactus Moon Publications. A huge thank you to both ladies.

Table of Contents

Part One: Ellen is an Advocate for the Beauty

Part Two: Ellen and the Dictator

Part Three: Ellen finds the Soldier

Part One

Ellen is an
Advocate
for Beauty

Chapter One: September 1958

I open the front door of our house. Flamboyant Miss Mamie flutters up the steps in her red, floral dress, balancing on one hand a gold scalloped tray overflowing with deviled eggs. "Oh, child," she says, placing her free hand on my shoulder, "How are we ever gonna live with this tragedy? You poor baby. Nothing much worse than losing your mama."

"Hello, Miss Mamie. Come on in." I take the eggs from her. I rearrange the casserole dishes on the dining room table to make room for the deviled eggs. Miss Mamie has followed me. As soon as I put the eggs down on the table, she enfolds me in her large, flabby arms. She smells to high heaven of Evening in Paris. I'm smothered.

As I turn to lead her to the living room to join the other ladies from the Esther Circle at the Marshall Methodist Church, I can't help hearing their whispers. "Do you think Ellen's mother drove off that bridge on purpose? I mean, Charlene's car just flew right off that bridge."

Miss Amy Taylor pipes in, "It's just all so tragic! How are Will and Ellen ever gonna live with this?"

"They're out here in the country with no next-door neighbor," says someone.

"Ellen's just a child," another says in a hushed voice.

The Methodist ladies turn in unison to look at my father. He's talking to one of the local farmers and is oblivious to their looks. My dad is the local county extension agent, employed by the county government to help farmers increase crop production, prevent erosion, and eliminate pests. So many of the local farmers have come to express their sympathy. They have a great deal of respect for my dad.

"I hear Will's sister, Essie, is coming to live with them. Lord knows," Miss Ann says, "Will's gonna need help with a seventeen-year-old girl."

"You know, I just don't think Charlene has looked happy for some time." Miss Nell squirms her bottom and sits up a little taller in her chair. "This whole mystery of Charlene's death is a conundrum."

"Ellen, don't listen to the old biddies. You know how they love to talk," Liz says, pulling me away from the drone of the women. Liz always says just what she means. We've been best friends since third grade. Liz knows all my deep dark secrets. She and Aunt Zia.

I try to take in what the Methodist ladies have said. I'm hurting. I didn't know that you could hurt like this and still survive. Did Mother drive her car off that bridge intentionally? Imagine how desperate she must have been if she did that. I can't fit desperation into a description of my mother.

The doorbell rings again. I mouth across the room to my father: "I'll get it." Gosh, everyone in the town of Marshall, Alabama, must already be in our living room. I wonder who else could be coming.

I open the door. It's Jo Jo Reed. Jo Jo lives down the road in one of the tenant houses on my grandfather's land. We're both seniors at Marshall High School. I've known Jo Jo all my life and have never seen him more uncomfortable. He's sliding his right work shoe back and forth in the dirt by the front steps. He's hanging his head, staring at the shoe. He looks miserable.

Jo Jo is a piece of work. Half the girls in Marshall County are in love with him. He's built like the jock he is. A dimple shows up in his right cheek when he smiles, but there is no dimple today. Jo Jo raises his head and looks me in the eye. His deep brown eyes are drooping with sorrow.

"Ellen—Sorry doesn't cut it. Don't know what to say."

I reach both arms around him and hug him. We just stand there, hugging each other. Finally, I say, "Come in and speak to Dad."

I leave Jo Jo with Dad and go to my bedroom, closing the door behind me. I have to be alone for a minute. I wonder if I'm having an out-of-body experience. I watch all the action swirling through the house. I know my mother is dead, but it doesn't seem real. Her Chevrolet flew off the Patterson Bridge and plummeted forty feet into the depths of Moore Creek. She's gone.

Dad and I have survived the hearing of it, and all the preparations for the funeral. Even the funeral itself. We have been surrounded by people ever since we heard the news, flowing from one day into the next in a blur. We've done the right things, said the right things. I'm outside myself. It doesn't feel real. Oh, hell! I'm a mess.

My father needs me. I make my way back to the crowd of people from Marshall filling up our living room. If casseroles and deviled eggs could make the pain go away, Dad and I would be flying high.

Dad talks to Aunt Eleanor, my mother's sister. I can tell he's hurting, too. I see it in the tight lines around his eyes and mouth. I slide up to him and tuck myself under his arm, listening to their plans.

Dad says, "Yes, Eleanor, I think that Essie is a good solution. She's been living by herself over on Nichols Street for thirty something years. Got to be lonely in that big house all by herself. It'll probably be good for all of us if she comes to live out here in the country."

"Hell, no!" I think. I almost say it out loud.

Essie is my father's sister. She's in her forties, totally out of touch with my world. Aunt Essie insists in ending everything she says in a Bible verse.

I think of the difference between Aunt Essie and Aunt Zia. What would I do without Zia? Granddaddy Callander named Aunt Zia during his "turning to the Jewish faith" period. We're Methodists but, from time to time, Granddaddy Callander entertains the notion of other religions. All my life, Aunt Zia has showered me with love.

Zia. Her name means "light" or "splendor"—appropriate words to describe my aunt. I adore this polished, honorable, highly energetic lady who is dedicated to her career. Someday I will be a broadcast journalist like Aunt Zia.

Aunt Zia was inspired by Nancy Dickerson, one of the first television news reporters. She met Nancy while working as a researcher with the Senate Foreign Relations Committee. Both of them fell in love with politics and were intrigued by the idea of presenting the workings of government to the public. When Nancy got her break and was hired by CBS News Bureau in Washington to produce "The Leading Question," a radio show that aired live interviews with politicians, she took Aunt Zia with her. Zia researched the politicians and prepared the interview questions. Nancy and Zia got to know almost all the senators and representatives in Washington.

Aunt Zia was on vacation in London in February 1952

when King George VI died suddenly and Queen Elizabeth II was formally proclaimed Queen of England. King George lay in state in Westminster Abbey for four days, from February 11 until February 15. During these days, Zia filed reports for various CBS broadcasts. She wrote about the life of King George, the reactions to his death, and the coronation that would be held before summer. When she came back to the United States, Aunt Zia knew that she had found her career.

Thank goodness, she came down from DC as soon as she heard the news about Mother. I look across the room to where she is standing and say a silent prayer of gratitude for Aunt Zia. I do have to smile when I think about the chaos she brings with her. She takes over the guest room, and Holy Moly! Any room Aunt Zia occupies just screams out, "Help! Invasion! Invasion!"

Her patent leather shoes and alligator heels are stacked by the closet door in the far corner of the bedroom. Hats are displayed on Styrofoam heads that line the bookcase—a row of sophisticated, bodiless women with no mouths. The dresser top in Aunt Zia's room is covered with boxes of face powder, artificial flowers, and bottles of May Cove perfume. Her closet is overflowing with furs and suits suitable for mourning. What Aunt Zia calls her work clothes—straight skirts and silk blouses with tissue-stuffed sleeves—hang neatly beside the suits.

I can see myself in those work clothes one day, tall and slim with my blue eyes and straight, blonde hair, holding the microphone like Aunt Zia. My always-a-little-crooked smile is visible as I tag the story, "Ellen Jones, CBS News. Marshall, Alabama."

The day drags on, and eventually the people begin to fade away with promises of still more casseroles and neighborly love to come. I listen to the crunching sound as the cars drive down the long gravel road that leads to our house.

Aunt Zia, Aunt Essie, Dad, and I sit down in the kitchen of our house. Not one of us can speak. The house is wrapped in total silence. I finally get up and go to my room without a word.

Our house is situated just outside the town of Marshall on plantation land that belongs to my grandfather, David Henry Callander. David Henry is one of those men that other men respect. The workers on the plantation look up to him just as the men in Marshall do, coming out to seek his advice on various matters.

Callander is a magical place. The sprawling plantation consists of a grist mill, a commissary, a syrup mill, a sawmill, a blacksmith shop, a cotton gin, and nearly 1,200 acres of rich farmland with fertile, coffee brown soil. The Linley River forms the land's eastern border. On the west side is Morgan Creek, which was dammed to furnish power to the grist mill and the cotton gin in operation here since the late 1800s. My grandfather makes enough cane syrup and cures enough meat from this land to feed his family and the eleven tenant families that live on the plantation. We live up the road from Callander proper, but I spend a lot of my time at the old plantation house.

Our house is a four-bedroom, one-bath, brick home about a mile from the plantation house. I suppose our house is insignificant compared to the Callander plantation house, which sits in the middle of the property and reigns from atop a high hill. Mother was never into decorating. Everything in our house is strictly functional, except the water. The water comes from a spring, and sometimes lizards and other reptiles find their way down the pipe and crawl right out the spigot into the tub. When we heard Mother scream, we knew another reptilian companion had made its way into the bathtub.

The best thing about our house is my bedroom. Every time I look at my room I think this room should be on the cover of

House Beautiful. All the furniture is cast off from Callander. Originally, none of the pieces matched, but I have painted each piece myself with a soft green paint called Forest of Ferns. Now, they are a finished set. The curtains and bedspread are sparkling white. The dresser top and bookcases provide a space for the display of family pictures: my mother in her college years, my Dad with his latest model car, and Aunt Zia traveling through Europe. I created this room, and it is one of the places where I can go to be by myself—to roll things around in my head.

Sitting down on my bed, I reach for my baby book, buried in the bottom drawer of my bedside table. Its edges are worn from all the times I've poured through it. I read my mother's beautiful cursive writing: *Ellen Jones was born in Marshall at Riverside Hospital on October 1, 1940.*

There are inked prints of my not-so-delicate feet and silhouettes of my face, hand-drawn and carefully cut out of the jet-black paper by Mother. I see once again that I had chicken pox when I was three and measles when I was nine. My mother has tenderly noted my first words and funny things I did in my early years. As I shift on my bed, a sheet of paper flutters softly out of the baby book and falls at my feet.

There on the page are Luella's predictions for me. Even the most intelligent, learned parents in our town go to Old Luella to predict the paths of their children's lives. The time-worn sheet contains her predictions for me, Ellen Jones, born to Will and Charlene Jones on the first day of October. I've read them over and over through the years, and still they make no sense to me.

Luella claims to have the eye to see the future. She has always scared us kids to death. Her stringy, gray hair and fingernails that curve in swirls, not to mention her warts, would scare anyone away—even before they knew how she makes her livelihood. She walks all stooped over down the streets of

Marshall. We always cross to the other side of the street to avoid
the strange and mysterious woman. Luella lives in a little house
on Culver Street. Supposedly, the house belonged to her father,
the local town doctor in the late 1800s.

I look down at her predictions for me. There are three:

She will be an advocate for the beauty.

She will find the soldier.

She will foil a dictator.

No matter how many times I read the predictions, I am
puzzled by them. I can't imagine being involved with a dictator,
and what soldier will I find? What the heck does "be an
advocate for the beauty" mean?

I hear a knock on my bedroom door. I close the baby book
softly. "Come in," I say.

Essie enters into my room with short, hesitant steps. As
usual, Aunt Essie is wearing a bib apron with faded spring
flowers all over it. Aprons are a permanent part of Essie as are
her laced-up walking shoes and salt-and-pepper hair that springs
from her head in tight curls, the results of the permanents she
gets every other month.

She closes her hand around the bedpost and leans toward
me. "Listen, Ellen. I'm not much for words. I want you to know
I'll do my best to help you and Will." She looks back over her
shoulder as she turns to leave and says, "Is any suffering like
my suffering. . .Lamentation 1:12." Essie leaves, and I am
enveloped by the silence.

My mother. I have to think about her now. I can't believe
she's gone. What about what the Methodist ladies said? Was my
mother unhappy? What do they mean "it wasn't an accident?"

There are so many questions inside me; I don't know where to start or what to think.

Mother once worked in the registrar's office at Marshall College. She was the artistic one in our family. She loved to sketch, and she wrote poetry. She fluttered through our lives, making sure that we had the proper clothes and ate healthy meals. She took care of our souls. I never knew her when she was not rushing from place to place and thing to thing. She was always full of life—and happy. I'd swear that she was happy. I rarely had a heart-to-heart talk with her though. Those were reserved for Aunt Zia. Mother was busy taking care of things. Aunt Zia was always ready to listen. That's the way things were.

I get ready for bed. My worn, flannel gown slides over my tired body. I turn off the light and scooch down under the comforter. It's the end of the longest day of my life.

The next morning Aunt Zia wakes me up when she sticks her head in my room. "Hey, Ellen. Get up, get up, girl. Essie has fixed breakfast. After we eat, we'll walk up to the grave."

I know Aunt Zia means the grave of Jonas Stockman, a revolutionary war soldier who died in 1839. No one knows a thing about Jonas Stockman. The grave my grandfather discovered years ago stands alone on Callander land. Aunt Zia and I like to visit the grave and make up stories about who Jonas actually was.

On our walk, I ask Aunt Zia about Mother. I explain what I heard the Methodist ladies say. Aunt Zia's response is reserved, which is unusual for her. She agrees. Something *was* bothering my mother. I want to know more but don't ask.

Most people put flowers on graves. Aunt Zia and I bring rocks to the soldier's grave. In ancient times, graves were marked with cairns, piles of rocks. The tradition of placing rocks may have originated as a way to build the cairn. Aunt Zia taught me this. The rocks show that people have visited the grave and that they care. We like rocks. They are permanent. There's not much in life that's permanent, I think.

Aunt Zia walks back to the house, leaving me at the grave alone. I read the tombstone again:

REVOLUTIONARY WAR SOLDIER

JONAS STOCKMAN

BORN 1753 DIED 1829

TRUTH AND HONOR

Truth and Honor. Every time I come to Jonas Stockman's grave, I'm touched by the words inscribed as a tribute to the soldier. What a person Jonas must have been. I think of Mother. My bright and shining mother. Was she a person of honor? I really need to know. The question haunts me more than ever as the questions surrounding her death hang in the air unanswered. If I find out that Mother was stained in some way, does that stain spread to me? I need to know the truth about Mother. Who was she, really? Who am I in light of who she was?

On the way back to the house, I detour by the family cemetery and visit the grave of Amanda Oglesby Callander, my maternal grandmother. As far as I know, she was the one true love of David Henry Callander. Amanda and David met when Amanda was teaching school in Marshall in 1892, and their courtship began that year. Her tombstone, etched with a death date of 1922, is nestled in with other Callander tombstones. She was just 48 years old when she died of influenza. I gently place a rock on her grave and say a silent prayer of gratitude that she was my grandmother.

The next morning, I join Dad and Aunt Essie at the kitchen table. Essie is reading *The Marshall Times-Standard*, and they are discussing an article about the death of a man named John Maben. "Essie, you remember—John Maben worked in the library at Marshall College in the 1930s," says Dad. "He was convicted of murdering a student, Ann Carson, in April of 1938 and sentenced to life in prison."

Essie replies, "That's all here in the paper. He died in prison some days ago of a heart attack. Everybody in Marshall has been talking about it."

I look over Dad's shoulder and see a picture of the murdered girl. Ann Carson was beautiful. She had long, brown hair that rippled in waves to her shoulder. Her eyes were large and soulful. She reminds me of Ava Gardner.

Aunt Essie says, "You shall not murder. Exodus 20:13."

Aunt Zia walks in with both arms full of hat boxes. She's leaving today to return to Washington. I already miss her. She looks me in the eye and says, "Ellen, don't forget to keep up ✗ with the world. When your father watches the news at night, you watch, too."

Of course, I'll watch the news. I want to be a reporter in the worst way. Really, I can't imagine *not* being a television news reporter. What would I do? Stay in Marshall? Marry? Have children? Join the Daughters of the American Revolution? I ✗ want so much more. I'm itching to get at it.   *Dream*

Chapter Two: October 1958

The evening news is a holy ritual in our house. Everyone has to sit quietly during the entire fifteen-minute newscast. Heaven forbid that we utter one word. Originally, we watched *The Camel News Caravan* hosted by John Cameron Swayze. Swayze wrote his own scripts and memorized them. No Teleprompters. The entertaining Swayze always opened his shows by saying, "Let's go hopscotching the world for headlines."

We sat mesmerized as we watched interviews with children of the South talking about desegregation. Chet Huntley and David Brinkley replaced Swayze in 1956, and we now hear international news from Chet Huntley in New York and national news from David Brinkley in Washington. Once I hear "Good night, Chet," followed by "Good night, David, and good night for NBC News," I am free to talk, thank goodness.

Since there is no news on Saturday, those nights are reserved for "Your Hit Parade." A regular group of vocalists—Dorothy Collins, Snooky Lanson, and Gisele MacKenzie—sing the seven most popular songs of the week. To make the show exciting, songs are sung in ascending order, with the number one song being sung last. Each Saturday night, I wait with bated breath to see what song will be number one. It bothers me the songs don't always sound like the originals. But, then again, it's hard for Gisele MacKenzie to sound like Fats Domino.

I love to hang out at the plantation house. On this particular day, all five feet and eight inches of me is draped over a rocking chair on the front porch. I am oblivious to all around me as I read the weekly edition of *The Marshall Times-Standard*.

I especially love the social notes: "Mrs. Lucy Stanford and her daughter, Amanda, spent Sunday afternoon visiting Mrs. R.C. Morris. They sat on the front porch and drank iced tea. Topics of conversation included The Singing Sims Sisters, who sang at church that morning, and Mrs. Stanford's son, Joe, who has a new job at The Piggly Wiggly."

In more a more serious article, I read that twenty colored people boarded buses in Birmingham, Alabama, on October 20 in protest of segregation. Thirteen were arrested, including Fred Shuttlesworth, who had declared in 1956 that colored members of the Alabama Christian Movement for Human Rights would desegregate Birmingham buses themselves if the city did not take action to do so.

I hate these stories of segregation. Why should the color of your skin prevent you from riding in the front of a bus or eating in any restaurant that you want to or, for gosh sakes, drinking from any water fountain? On Saturdays, the sidewalks of Marshall are overflowing with people, colored and white. But they don't mix. Water fountains on the side of the courthouse are labeled *White* and *Colored*. Whites go eat in the downtown restaurants—colored people do not. The white Baptist church is on one side of the street and the African Methodist Episcopal Church is across the street. I see these things in Marshall, but it's not like that on Callander land. My Grandfather sees to that.

When I hit junior high, Grandfather set out to teach me about racial hatred. It was then I learned that life on Callander was not the norm. I had to read and discuss with him: *The Diary of a Young Girl, Black Boy* by Richard Wright, and *Annie Allen*, a book of poems by Gwendolyn Brooks that earned her the Pulitzer Prize back in 1950.

I look up to see Mr. Wilson, chairman of the school board, shuffling up the steps. He says, "Hi there, Ellen Jones. How's the world treating you?" Mr. Wilson always asks this question in just the same way, "How's the world treating you?" I always answer, "Wonderfully well, Mr. Wilson."

"You're a senior in high school this year?" he asks.

"Yes, sir," I answer.

"Mr. Dave in?" Mr. Wilson is here to see my grandfather. I tell him to go right in to my grandfather's study.

I can't help but overhear my grandfather and Mr. Wilson talking. Actually, Mr. Wilson is talking. My grandfather is listening. Mr. Wilson is reviewing all the year's school events. My ears perk up when I hear him mention Neta Levy. He's talking about the Miss Marshall County High School Beauty Pageant.

"Well, Mr. Dave, I'm hearing a lot of talk about this Neta Levy. Hear that she's a real beauty. I'm telling you right now, we can't have a Jewish girl as Miss Marshall County High. Everyone knows your granddaughter, Ellen, will probably win. Still, some of us don't even want Neta in the pageant."

This beauty pageant is set up in a weird way. Different high school clubs, classes, and sports teams sponsor beauties. Professional-looking, 8x10 glossies are made of each girl, and these pictures are sent to *The Mobile Press-Register,* where the editor and staff members at the paper select the finalists. The student body then votes on a winner from these finalists, and the winner is crowned at The Miss Marshall High School Beauty Pageant in March.

How ignorant can adults be? Why can't a Jewish girl be the local beauty pageant winner? Who wants to be a beauty pageant winner, anyway? The questions swirl around in my head.

I see myself producing stories about social injustice. "This is Ellen Jones live on the air—" My mind floats as I think of possibilities in my future. I tilt my head back and smell the honeysuckle vine permeating the air. The four o'clock flowers are wide open to the sunshine. These bushes get their name from the fact that all the flowers close up into buds like tiny knots every afternoon.

I jerk back to reality as I hear the raised voice of my grandfather. I have never in my life heard him shout, but he's shouting now. "Damn you, Mr. Wilson. I'll have no hand in keeping this Neta girl out of the pageant or out of anything else. How can you even think about doing this?"

I sit up straight just as Mr. Wilson strides out the front door, crosses the front porch, and marches down the steps. He looks like an emperor penguin as he furiously shuffles down the worn steps and waddles toward his Chevy Impala. He hops in his car hastily and roars down the drive. My grandfather doesn't know I'm still on the porch. I don't want him to know I've overheard the conversation, so I quickly jump off the end of the porch and make a beeline in the direction of home.

I find Aunt Essie cleaning the house from top to bottom. That means I'm cleaning as well. Aunt Zia is coming back this weekend, and no one is more excited than me. Before I know it, she is back at Callendar again. She has come to help clear out my mother's things.

We're sitting in the dining room with pictures and memorabilia spread out all over the table. One box holds pictures of Mother and Dad's wedding. I smile as I remember Mother telling me about Grandfather Callander's wedding gift—a white, square box filled with one hundred silver dollars. Mother and Daddy started out with little or no money, and

Daddy had to pay for their honeymoon with the silver dollars. I laugh as I think of Dad paying for their hotel room at the Grand Hotel in Point Clear, Alabama, with a box of silver dollars. Mother said that Dad's face was as red as the wine they drank the night before. The Grand Hotel is all that the name implies, having been around since the 1800s and catering to the wealthiest citizens of Alabama. It was, and still is, the ultimate destination for honeymooners in our state.

Aunt Zia and I find another box is stuffed full of pictures of me when I was a baby. Many of the pictures show Mother holding me. In my favorite, she seems to be singing to me. I ache when I look at the pictures and close the lid quickly. I open the last box, not knowing what I will find. It's filled with pictures of Mother during her college days. Long before she started working on campus, Mother attended Marshall College herself. I pick up a handful of pictures.

There she is: Mother and a girl with long brown hair that ripples in waves to her shoulder. Her eyes are large and soulful. She reminds me of Ava Gardner. Suddenly, I know I have seen her before. In the newspaper article. She is Ann Carson. I am shocked to see that my mother knew the murdered girl. I never heard Mother mention her, but it seems from the pictures that they were close friends. I ask Aunt Zia about this. She should know whether Mother was friends with the dead girl.

Aunt Zia doesn't seem to want to talk about Ann Carson but confirms Mother and Ann were college roommates. This sends shock waves through my system, but I change the subject and talk to Aunt Zia instead about Neta Levy. She tells me to write about it. We talk about hard news, which I have learned is the factual accounting of a current event or breaking events, such as earthquakes or the election of President Eisenhower. We talk about soft news which, unlike hard news, is not time-sensitive. The profile of a person is an example of soft news. She tells me about editorials, which allows the writer to express their own opinion or point of view.

Aunt Zia has me read aloud the stories I write over and over. She preaches, "Ellen, you are writing for the ear. It has to sound right." She teaches me to write in active voice and to write in short sentences. An example of active voice is: President Lincoln delivered the Gettysburg Address—not: The Gettysburg Address was delivered by President Lincoln. I'll add all this information to the notebook I'm making. My notebook has all sorts of information about broadcast journalism, from how to compose shots to how to write a script.

We continue to look at pictures as, in my mind, I compose the beginning of an editorial about Neta Levy. I take a break from going through Mother's things and head for my room so I can put to paper the editorial that's already forming in my head. With all Granddaddy has taught me about racial hatred, I am not about to sit still for what Mr. Wilson wants to do. I finish the editorial and read my finished work:

Who is the fairest of them all? The Mobile Press-Register staff will never find Neta Levy to be one of the fairest. She will not compete to be crowned. She will not get a chance to hear the roar of the crowd at Marshall County High as she walks across the stage. Why? Because she is Jewish.

Neta and her family have lived in Marshall since the late forties. Her grandparents came from Germany, and they settled in Mobile. Her grandfather started his business by selling house to house. He saved enough money to buy a cart and then, finally, rented a storefront for his mercantile business.

Ten years later, he bought the store. Wooman's was

a Mobile landmark for seventy years. In 1952, Neta's
father moved to Marshall to open another branch of
the well-respected clothing store. The Levys are
contributing citizens of Marshall.

We cry aloud in horror and frustration at the
atrocities committed on the Jewish race in Germany
and Poland during World War II. The Jews were forced
to wear yellow stars and live in ghettos, shuttled off
to concentration camps where they were gassed and
buried in mass graves. We agree that that could never
happen in our country. "Not in our town," we say.

Racism

Neta will not wear the yellow star, but she will
be discriminated against, nonetheless. Neta should be
a contestant in The Miss Marshall County High School
Beauty Pageant. By all accounts, she is one of the most
beautiful girls at the school.

Racism

Contestants are nominated by classes, sports
teams, and clubs. The finalists of the pageant are
determined by The Mobile Press-Register editor and
staff. However, the school board chairman will not
send Neta's photo to The Mobile Press-Register if she
is nominated.

The sole reason? Neta is Jewish.

Racism

What a travesty! I suggest that, in the future,
the Marshall County High students and teachers
handle the pageant with no input from the Board
of Education. I further suggest the student body be
allowed to vote on the contestants, selecting a winner
from live contestants, not by reviewing 8x10 glossies
sent off to the Mobile newspaper.

So, who is the fairest of them all? In my book,

it's Neta Levy. The students of Marshall High School may or may not crown her, but she should be allowed to compete. The school board's exclusion of her based on her heritage is nothing short of bigotry and must be corrected.

Chapter Three: November 1958

The next day is Saturday. Zia leaves in a flurry, and, as usual, I go to town with Dad. Our routine is to go into Marshall on Saturday afternoons. We've done this as long as I can remember, and the tradition continues even though Mother is gone.

Today, I have several favorite places to go: the library, the drugstore, and *The Marshall Times-Standard* building. I need to talk to Lewis Henry, the owner and current editor of our town paper. Mr. Henry's office is on the main floor. He asks me to pull up a rickety stool to the long work board where he's seated. He's going through photographs for the next edition. He has a passion for photojournalism. When he has time, he talks to me about photographs.

Mr. Henry hands me a photograph and says, "Look at this one, Ellen. It's a close-up. Look at the wonderful details—the deep trenches in the face, the path the tear takes as it runs down the face, and the look of despair in his eyes."

I look at the photograph Mr. Henry is holding and understand the power of such a shot. I pick up another picture and say, "What about this one, Mr. Henry?"

"Why, Ellen, that's a long shot. Some people call it a wide shot. This photograph shows the little girl, but it does more than that. It establishes the scene and shows us where she is." He leans in closer. "We know that she's on a working farm. See the farm equipment? Look at all those animals—chickens, guineas, pigs, and goats. They use these shots at the beginning of movies to show where the action is taking place."

We look at more photos while I work up the courage to ask Mr. Henry what I really want. I want to look in the archives for the papers from 1936. I finally just ask Mr. Henry if I can go through the papers stacked in the archives.

"Sure, Ellen," he says. "Just let me know if you need help. Papers are stacked by year and month."

I thank him and head to the back room, where the archives are located. I pull out the June, July, and August 1936 editions of *The Marshall Times-Standard*. The first thing that I notice is a bunch of advertisements. The cigarette ad catches my eye first—*For digestion's sake, smoke Camels* it reads.

The third edition in the month of July features a front-page story on the murder trial verdict. The best hard news stories open with a lead that contains the four W's and may also include why and how. I remember that one or more of these may be understood. I break the Maben story down that way and see it's all here except for how.

Who: John Maben; worked as head librarian at the Marshall College Library

What: April 12, pronounced guilty of murder in the first-degree of Ann Carson, found strangled in the rose garden located at the president's home on the Marshall College campus. Maben is sentenced to life in prison.

Where: Marshall County Courthouse

When: July 21, 1936

Why: Maben's guilty verdict was based on the testimony of Loraine Hudson, the college president's wife, who testified that she saw John Maben standing

over the body of Ann Carson at 10:00 p.m. on the night
of April 12. John Maben's wife, Deborah, testified
that Maben was home with her that night.

There's no indication in the story that my mother would be involved in any way. I'm relieved, but something is still bothering me. The whole thing's such a mystery, and Ann was Mother's roommate. It's not a stretch to think Mother may have known something. I make notes on the article and say goodbye to Mr. Henry.

Back at school on Monday, I head straight for the *Voice* office before class. I'm the editor for Marshall High's school newspaper. I'm the editor, so I have the key. I pull the silver key out of my purse and insert it in the lock. As always, I get that special feeling of achievement curling in my stomach. I walk through the door and see a note taped to the overhead projector. Miss Taylor is out with a virus. But Miss Taylor is never sick! It is frustrating that I can't show her my editorial today.

My first class is Algebra Two, taught by Miss Rebecca. I love the problem-solving of algebra. As I walk in the door, I hear everyone talking about the pageant.

Mable Johnson, the mayor's daughter, is bragging. "I'm on the planning committee, and this year's pageant is gonna be the best."

Neta Levy is sitting on the back row. I look at her carefully. She seems oblivious to the fact she will never compete.

Mable spots me and says, "Well, Ellen. I'm sure you think you'll win."

I am not a Mable Johnson fan. She always has to be better than me. Every boy that I like, she likes. Every club that I join, she joins. I've heard that she's spreading rumors about my mother committing suicide. She's a real bitch!

All the ancestors are spinning as I use the B-word, even if it is only in my thoughts. Young ladies never curse. I ignore Mable, as usual, but Liz walks into the room and hears her. Liz can't resist a comeback.

"Why, Mable," she drawls, "It's a sure thing that you'll never win. You'll have to get your Dad to sponsor you. Humph! I think that you have to be thin to be a pageant winner."

Liz looks Mable up and down, sits down by me, and hands me my slam book. Everyone in the senior class is doing slam books this year. They are spiral notebooks with the senior's name on the first page and two columns of numbers, one through thirty-nine, on the second page. A blank line is placed to the right of each number. Thirty-nine is the number of graduates in our class. The rest of the pages in the slam books have one question at the top of each page.

Any senior who signs your slam book signs their name in the blank by a number on the second page. Then, they answer the questions in your slam book by putting their number and their answer to each question. Slam books can be nasty, but mine has questions like, "Who is your favorite rock group?" or "Who in our class will grow up to be president?" Liz is the first to sign my book.

When I get home that afternoon, Aunt Essie tells me Aunt Zia called. She has been assigned by CBS to interview Fulgencio Batista, president of Cuba. She is flying to Havana tomorrow along with a cameraman where she will interview this president with ties to the American Mafia.

Aunt Essie, Dad, and I talk about nothing but Aunt Zia at dinner that night. Dad has actually been to Havana. He and Mother went when I was eight. Dad tells us about going to a cabaret called the Tropicana, where they saw Nat King Cole perform. He tells us the grounds of the Tropicana are beautifully landscaped, and dancers perform on catwalks in the trees. I'm excited for Aunt Zia. "The land you are entering to possess is a land polluted by the corruption of its peoples. Ezra 9:11," Aunt Essie pronounces.

The next day I'm back at the door of the *Voice* room, silver key in hand, but it turns out I don't need the key today. Glorious, wonderful Miss Taylor is there. I imagine Miss Taylor hearing the old saying constantly in her childhood: "I'd rather be dead than red on the head." Her hair is a long, tangled mass of red. Half of her face is covered with purple-rimmed eyeglasses. The other half is turned up in a smile. I love her.

I tell her all about the editorial I have in mind. I start with Mr. Wilson's visit to my grandfather and end by reading her my rough draft. I explain that I want to print the editorial in *The Voice*. Her smile vanishes.

"Ellen Jones, there is no way you can print that. The school board, the principal, and most of the teachers will pitch the worst hissy fit you've ever seen. I'll be fired, and you, who hope to be valedictorian of your class, will never graduate."

Racism

We stare at each other in silence. I give in. I roll my editorial up and walk out of the room. I'm not happy with myself. I didn't fight for this. Worse, I didn't fight for Neta Levy. *Truth and Honor*. The phrase rolls around in my mind, and I fear I'm a failure.

Truth & Honor

Saturday comes, and I think of Aunt Eleanor. I don't see her often, but she was in college with Ann Carson and Mother. She may know something I want to know. I decide to invite myself for tea. Aunt Eleanor lives in the president's home on Marshall College's campus. She's married to John Glover, president of Marshall College.

I love any occasion to walk through front campus. Even with all the leaves off the trees, it's beautiful—stark, but still beautiful. The tall, Greek Revival-style library rises from the lawn on the left of front campus. The two-story library features a front entry porch bordered with four tall columns on either side. Plain pilasters and narrow windows tinted in cranberry, blue, green, and yellow flank the front door. The library houses an impressive section of books and monographs on the history of Marshall. I've spent many afternoons curled up in one of two large, overstuffed chairs reading about Marshall as it existed long ago.

Just past the library, I turn right in front of the main dorm, Reynolds Hall. I survey the four round columns, each topped with a long pediment. I know there are twenty windows in the main section of Reynolds. I counted them as a child whenever I came to campus to see Mother. The main section has a recessed wing on each side, and each wing contains ten windows. I loved looking at those windows and wondering what was inside.

I walk past the front of the building and arrive at my favorite building on campus, the president's house. The president's house is called Rose Hall because it has an extensive rose garden in the rear of the house. Roses bloom in abandon along the edge of a maze of boxwoods. Roses are also planted in front of the house.

Inside, I call out for Aunt Eleanor. The epitome of a genteel southern lady, she invites me into the front parlor. She wears straight, long skirts with black or brown heels, and she's never without her pearl earrings and necklace perfectly positioned over her silk blouse. Her long hair is shaped into a chignon at the base of her neck.

Aunt Eleanor fixes her light blue eyes on me and tells me again how sorry she is about Mother. After we talk about Aunt

Essie moving in and Aunt Zia making the trip to Cuba, I tell her that I ran across pictures of Mother and Ann Carson while going through Mother's things.

"I'm curious about Ann Carson. What do you remember about her?"

Aunt Eleanor just looks at me for a moment.

"Ann and Charlene were great friends all through college," she says. "They even roomed together their last two years on campus. If you've seen the pictures, you know Ann was quite the beauty." She continues, "The boys swarmed around her. She usually ignored them. Ann was different from most college girls—she couldn't care less about boys. She cared more about politics. She swore she would be the first woman governor of Alabama, and no one doubted she could fulfill that dream."

[handwritten margin note: The beauty ?]

Aunt Eleanor paused and looked up at me again. "Your mother, on the other hand—well—Charlene was just the opposite. She loved the boys and had no interest in a career. She just wanted a husband and children." She smiles as she remembers Mother. "They were very different, those two. You know, Ann worked in the president's office her senior year. I can hardly look at the rose garden in the back without thinking of her."

"Why was she so interested in politics?" I ask.

"She was raised by her aunt and uncle. Her uncle was a state senator in the early forties. She adored him."

"What did she do in the president's office?" I ask.

"Ann filed reports and other paperwork for Adam Hudson, the college president at that time."

I certainly know more about Ann Carson now but am still

surprised Mother never talked about her. I think I'll just let what Aunt Eleanor told me bubble around inside my head for a while. I move away from the topic of Ann Carson and talk to Aunt Eleanor about upcoming events in Marshall while we finish our tea.

After the visit with Aunt Eleanor, I visit *The Marshall Times-Standard* building. I spot Mr. Henry in the workroom. "Hi there, Mr. Henry. Ya got a minute to talk?"

"Always got time for you, Ellen."

"Mr. Henry, I was just over at the campus talking to Aunt Eleanor. We were talking about Ann Carson working in the president's office and about her murder." He looks surprised. I wait for his response.

"I always thought that whole thing was really strange," he says. "I can't see John Maben killing anyone. I remember the time so well. The campus was all in an uproar over the SACS Committee coming. Such a big deal. SACS is The Southern Association of Colleges and Schools, and they accredit regional schools by determining if they are meeting predetermined standards. I even wrote several articles about it. That was in April. Take another look at the back issues. That's 1936 if you're interested. Maybe you'll find something."

"I may do that the next time I stop by the paper," I say.

I turn to walk out the door. Before I get out, Mr. Henry calls after me: "What do hear from your Aunt Zia?"

"We've heard from her several times," I tell him. "She's still in Cuba. She was assigned to do one interview with Batista, but then CBS asked her to stay and finish a series of interviews."

"It seems that she's been there forever," Mr. Henry says.

"Aunt Zia met a sugar cane plantation owner who she mentions in all her letters. David Foca is his name. I think that he's one of the reasons she's still in Cuba." I smile. "High drama."

I say goodbye to Mr. Henry and head home. The dramas in my young life, besides Mother's death, which is a drama that plays constantly in my head, involve high school and the swirling life taking place there. Recently, the Miss Marshall Beauty Pageant and Neta Levy have been at the forefront of my high school worries, but today the National Honor Society has nudged Neta and all the other worries aside for a moment.

The National Honor Society taps its new members before Christmas, and I want to be a member. The society honors students who have demonstrated excellence in the areas of scholarship, leadership, service, and character—and talk about drama—that's a National Honor Society tapping! Everyone in the high school is seated in the school auditorium, and parents of the students being tapped are in the audience. If you see a parent in the group, you know right away their student will make it.

It is Monday afternoon when I enter the auditorium—jam-packed because the whole school attends along with the superintendent and the school board. I see Mable Johnson's parents. I do not see my father or Aunt Essie anywhere. Damn.

But wait! There's Jo Jo Reed's father. He's wearing a freshly starched, long-sleeved, white shirt, overalls, and his work shoes. He stands out in this room of well-dressed people who have worn their Sunday best for this important occasion. I walk up and speak to him. I'm so excited about Jo Jo being in the National Honor Society. I only wish I could be in it with him.

The program begins. Existing members give the invocation and tell about the history of the Marshall organization. They talk about the requirements needed to be a member. Then, the tapping begins. Members seated on the stage come down the stage steps and walk, one at a time, through the audience. They have the responsibility of walking up behind the newly selected members seated in the audience and tapping them on the shoulder.

I groan as I see Mable Johnson tapped. I'm elated as I see Jo Jo tapped. Then I definitely feel the tap on my shoulder. I tremble and have to place my hands on both sides of my legs to push up off the chair. I stand up tall and follow the member who tapped me to the stage. Once I'm on stage, I see them. My dad, Aunt Essie, and Aunt Eleanor are right there on the second row! I couldn't see them from the back of the room. That feeling, almost a glow, moves through my body. I am thrilled.

After the ceremony, I am repeatedly hugged by family and Miss Taylor. I turn, and there she is: Mabel Johnson. I take the high road and congratulate her. She smirks. I turn the other way and see Jo Jo with his father. We bring them into our group, for they are members of our Callander clan.

We're leaving the auditorium to go back to class when Jo Jo grabs my arm. "Hey, Ellen," he whispers. "You're the best!" I give him a quick hug and am surprised at the way I feel—like maybe I want to hug him forever. He smiles at me. The dimple shows, and I'm totally flustered. Why am I feeling this way about Jo Jo?

Chapter Four: December 1958

Choosing a university is a tremendous decision—one of the most important that I'll make in this life. I've sorted through catalogs at the library and written to universities for others. I decide on The University of Columbus in Miami because of its broadcast journalism department. I can't declare a major until my junior year at the university and that's still three years away, but the George W. Newman College of Journalism at the University of Columbus includes a broadcast program that will allow freshmen and sophomores to work in minor roles on its nightly newscast.

That's a positive for the University of Columbus program. It is one of two schools in the United States that actually produces a newscast which airs to the college and the town where it is located. This is for me. First, I have to be accepted.

I stop working on the application when I hear Dad yell from the kitchen, "News from Aunt Zia."

I no sooner walk into the kitchen when Dad breaks the news. "She's married! She married David Foca, and they are living in a section of Havana called Miramar." Zia is known for her snap decisions—decisions that are usually perfectly suited to her.

Dad fills in the details. "Zia is giving us background information on the family. David has two children by a previous marriage. Carlota is fourteen, and Julio is thirteen," he says looking down at the letter. "David attended preparatory school in the United States and graduated from Columbia. Before going back to Cuba, Zia says he spent one year in New Orleans working in sugar refineries. Her new husband owns sugar cane plantations, mills, and refineries in Matanzas and Oriente provinces." Dad smiles.

"There is even more detail to report," he says. "Zia has written that each week the Focas catch the train in Havana and travel to an *ingenio*—the word used to describe the area that includes the office, sugar mill, sugar refinery, sugar fields, and the town where the workers reside. Zia and the children ride horses and watch the barefoot workers in the fields while David conducts business in the office."

 Zia has saved the best for last. "She's coming for Christmas—and she's bringing the children with her." I notice a change in Dad. Zia's coming excites him. When he turns his brown eyes in my direction, there's a sparkle in his eyes that hasn't been there since Mother died.

I really look at him. Before Mother died, he was always the well-dressed GQ man with stylish clothes and a spring in his step. This is not the man I see before me. How could I not have noticed? His pants with their tiny, checked pattern and his cotton dress shirt are wrinkled. His black wing-tipped shoes are scuffed. With the news of Aunt Zia's visit, some of the sparkle is back.

Dad's sparkle is contagious. Aunt Zia is coming! I'll make a million plans for us—we'll shop, we'll walk, and I'll tell her all about Columbus University. Suddenly, I have a burst of creative energy. I want to tackle the archives at *The Marshall Times-Standard* before Christmas, so I decide to leave the college applications and head out to see Mr. Henry.

"Hi, Ellen. You came to look in the archives or do you just want to visit an old man?"

"No old men around," I answer. "But I do want to look at the back papers."

"Help yourself," says Mr. Henry.

In the back room, I pull the April 1936 issues of the paper. The edges are worn, and the paper has yellowed over time. This issue is chock full of articles about the Southern Association of Colleges and Schools, or SACS for short, paying Marshall College a visit. Marshall has been placed on sanctions before, I read; therefore, it's critical that Marshall meet standards. If the college doesn't meet the accrediting agency's standards, the Southern Baptist Convention, which oversees the college, will take away funding. The college could be closed.

There are distinct disadvantages in attending a college that is not accredited. Federal loans are harder to obtain as are scholarships. Admittance to universities to receive advanced degrees is less likely for those who attend non-accredited schools, and some branches of the military require degrees from an accredited college. According to several articles, Marshall College departments, such as Biology, Chemistry, Mathematics, and English were focusing on reviewing the existing curricula, increasing the number of honor tracks available to students, and increasing the number of graduates.

The newspaper article reports methods of gathering evidence of success included student progress toward program-level outcomes, student achievement at the end of the course of study, and student scores on standardized tests. How nervous the college administration and staff must have been about the results of the SACS visit! Townspeople who were aware of the impact of the SACS visit must have been concerned about the results as well.

I think of Mother and all those pictures of her at college I have in my room. She worked at the college all her life. Think how her life would have been different if Marshall College had been forced to close. This SACS visit was a big deal in our little town.

Later editions of the paper applaud the success of President Adam Hudson and the faculty. It seems Marshall College met SACS standards after all and accomplished their goals and objectives. The articles are filled with pictures of President Hudson and his wife, Lorraine, who testified against John Maben at his trial.

So, Ann Carson was killed the week before the SACS Committee came to town. What a hectic time for Marshall! I place the papers in their proper place and return to the main workroom to say goodbye to Mr. Henry. Before I leave, he has to give me advice on my camera work. He wants me to work on shooting close-ups. He tells me to bring the viewer close to the emotion happening in the story. I promise to bring him shots to critique as I go out the front door.

On my way out, I stop in my tracks when I see the name on the office next door: Marshall County School Board. I make a snap decision to go in and speak to Mr. Wilson about Neta Levy. Miss Jenkins, who has been secretary to the chairman of the school board for eons, says, "Come on in, Ellen. What can we do for you?" If I were the school board chairperson, I'd want Miss Jenkins for my secretary. She's so gracious. Her hair is in a tidy, swirled bun, and her glasses, attached to a string of black beads, hang around her neck. She's wearing a high-necked, pink blouse with a tiny ruffle around the neck.

"Hi, Miss Jenkins. Is Mr. Wilson in?"

"He's in. I'll see if he can see you." She leaves for a moment to check with Mr. Wilson.

"Yes. He'll be glad to see you, Ellen."

I jump. I'm deep in thought and her voice startles me. I'm nervous. What am I doing?

With all the confidence I can muster, I confront Mr. Wilson in his office. "Good morning, Mr. Wilson. Do you have a minute? Something's on my mind that I'm really worried about." From behind his huge, mahogany desk, he motions for me to sit down, then leans in, and peers over his thick-rimmed glasses.

"I have a confession to make, Mr. Wilson." I am stumbling over the words already. "I overheard you tell my grandfather about not allowing Neta in the Miss Marshall pageant. I know that the pageant is not until March, but I can't get this off my mind. My grandfather was upset. I'm upset. Surely you won't keep Neta out."

Mr. Wilson replies, "Now Ellen, don't you worry your pretty little head about the Miss Marshall pageant. You're right. It's not until March."

"But I'm really upset about what you said to Grandfather. I've even written an editorial about it. How could you *think* about not allowing Neta in the pageant?"

"Aw, Ellen. You know I wouldn't do such a thing. Now you just run along and don't worry 'bout this." He smiles; his long, yellowed teeth disgust me. He has no intention of talking about Neta. *No need for further conversation.*

Of course, he's lying. I don't want to be around him. I get up from my seat and leave hastily.

"Goodbye, Miss Jenkins. Good to see you."

His voice seems to stalk me as I pick up my pace and round the corner. How could this man serve on the school board? He reminds me of a slimy, slithering snake. I can't believe men like my grandfather and my dad exist in the same world with people like Mr. Wilson.

On Main Street, the city workers are up on a ladder, hanging Christmas wreaths with red bows on every lamppost in town. Christmas is a coming! Most of the workers know me. "Merry Christmas!" Jim Bailey shouts down from his ladder. This Christmas will be extra special because Aunt Zia is coming and bringing Carlota and Julio with her. I wonder what the children will be like.

In Miss Ann's dress shop, I search for gifts for the aunts and Carlota. I've already bought a biography of Marguerite Higgins for Aunt Zia. Marguerite Higgins covered the Korean War and won a Pulitzer Prize for international reporting in 1951. I buy gloves for Aunt Essie and scarves for Aunt Eleanor and Carlota.

Next door, in the dime store, I hunt for a gift for Julio. I don't know Julio, and I have no idea what to buy for a thirteen-year-old boy. My eye falls on the Zorro Official Guitar. Only nine dollars—a bargain. A silhouette of Zorro has been painted on the face of the guitar, and the famous Z appears in several places. The Zorro guitar may not appear in the National Museum of Music, but something tells me that Julio will like it. I buy it.

With Christmas comes the annual Christmas pageant at the Methodist Church. Mother and Aunt Eleanor always directed it in the past. This year Liz and I are helping. The pageant costumes are always stored in our attic, and it's our job to get them to the church. I have always loved to walk up in the attic and see all the costumes. It's like Christmas is hanging out in our attic, just waiting to make an appearance.

As we carry the boxes down one by one, I remember my own experience in the pageant. I was always an angel. Mother had all of us angels packed into the narthex. We wore the white robes with gossamer wings and held lit candles. Outwardly poised, I was always secretly terrified that I'd set the angel ahead of me on fire.

Liz and I load the costumes into her car and drive them over to the church. We are the first to arrive. Glad the church is open; I love walking into the church sanctuary when no one is there. It's nice to feel God in the stillness. I go up to the altar rail and kneel. I say a prayer for Mother. Liz kneels beside me. She knows what I'm doing, and she gives my shoulder a quick squeeze.

Liz is an amazing friend. She's right there, helping when I'm down in a hole. And she makes me laugh when I'm not. "Hey, Ellen," she says. "Guess who has eyes for Jo Jo Reed?" She pauses for effect. "None other than Mable Johnson." I feel this tiny flutter in my stomach. I don't like the idea of Mable liking Jo Jo.

"I wish her luck with that one. On second thought, no I don't. Jo Jo is too nice for Mable."

Zia arrives with the children in time for the Christmas pageant and settles in with her many dresses, shoes, and hats. She has brought gifts, too, including several books in Spanish, for me. She wants me to open the books before Christmas, but Zia says I have to learn to count from one to a hundred in Spanish before I can open them. I get right to it. "Uno, dos, tres. . ."

Julio fits right in at the plantation. He spends mornings with Grandfather, asking endless questions about how the plantation runs. "What is cotton?" he asks. "How do you pick it? What is it used for?" He's fascinated with the tenants and follows them to the fields whenever Grandfather is not around.

I don't think Carlota wants to be here. She's a beautiful girl, and she's quite bright. But she argues—constantly argues. "The lamb is delicious," someone may say. She will say, "It's dry. I want chicken." In secret, Aunt Zia confides that she wants to scream. At the table, she just smiles at Carlota. "Maybe you are right," she says.

Carlota constantly compares life in Marshall to life in Cuba. One night at dinner, she asks about the local art museum. When told that Marshall has no art museum, she comments that she could never live in a place where she could not visit Raphael and Tomás Sánchez. Essie has a quick reply: "Do everything without complaining and arguing. Philippians 2:14."

Christmas morning before church, we open gifts. The aunts are appreciative of the gifts, and Dad loves the Mario Lanza record I bought for him. I get clothes from the aunts as well as another book from Aunt Zia—this one on interviewing skills. Julio seems to like the guitar. Carlota barely glances at the scarf. Dad surprises me. He gives me a necklace that belonged to Mother. I get that huge lump in my throat I always get when someone or something touches me deeply. I visualize Mother standing in front of her dresser while placing this very necklace around her neck. In my memory, she sees me and smiles.

"Thank you, Dad."

He can tell how much it means to me. He tries to lighten the mood. "Everybody, don't forget that we go to the plantation house tonight for David Henry's eggnog party!"

We walk in the great hall at Callander, and the eggnog is flowing. The nog on the left side of the room is for the ladies and the children. The nog on the right side of the room is for the men. The men's eggnog is seasoned with Jim Beam. That's why they're so happy, I think.

I give David Henry Callander a huge Christmas hug, standing on tip-toe to hug him. My grandfather is tall like all the Callanders before him. I speak to Jo Jo's dad and ask where Jo Jo is. "He's out back," Mr. Callander says.

Down the hall is the eight-foot cedar, decorated with Shiny Brite ornaments. There's not a tree in Marshall that doesn't have Shiny Brites on it. They are all the rage right now. I pass it and open the back door. Jo Jo is just coming in.

"Went back home," he tells me. "Have something for you." He hands me a flat box wrapped in Santa Claus wrapping paper and topped with a bright red stick-on bow. "I want you to open it now," he says. I open the box and almost drop the thin piece of paper.

"It's a poem for you. I wanted you to have something special from me this year." I stand in the dim light by the back door and read Jo Jo's poem. I can hardly swallow for the huge lump in my throat. I can't speak. I hug Jo Jo and that feeling is back. I just want to stand there with Jo Jo's arms around me forever.

Of course, I can't do that. Christmas is still with us and I have things to do. I always place a wreath on Jonas Stockman's grave at Christmastime. This year Aunt Zia helps me. We stand at the back door and ready ourselves for the hike to Jonas' grave. I slide my arms into my worn, red car coat and fumble with the one-inch long buttons that look like little wooden kegs. I top my ensemble with fluffy earmuffs that remind me of rabbit's fur. Hopefully the death of bunnies did not go into making these atrocious things that hurt my ears while keeping them warm. I look at Aunt Zia. She's wearing a stylish, bright blue full and swingy top coat with large, rolled-up sleeves, and is that a cashmere hat she's wearing? The lady is always voguish.

She tucks her arm through mine as we walk across the backyard into the woods. The earthy smell of decaying leaves mixed with the fresh smell of cedar trees slides up my nostrils. I love the woods; it has its own cast of characters. We see an opossum waddle across our path. When it sees us, it drops to the ground and curls up in a fuzzy circle. Playing dead, of course. No worries there for Mr. Opossum; I wouldn't touch him with the proverbial "ten-foot pole."

There are squirrels aplenty and, as we pass the small pond, we see the tip of a beaver's black, paddle-like tail as he dives to enter his mud-covered lodge. I'm always amazed that these rodents can fell a large tree.

I turn and smile at Aunt Zia. What a stunning picture she makes against the backdrop of stark, leafless hardwood trees. She's like a splash of color in a gray world. She smiles back.

Aunt Zia breaks the moment by asking, "So, what story will we make up about Jonas today?"

I think for a moment and say, "I know. He was a writer of western novels. You know, like Zane Grey."

"Then why is he buried in Alabama?" asks Zia.

I take a moment to think. I smile. "He came to Alabama to watch Andrew Jackson fight against the Red Stick Creek Indians. I'll bet he died in the battle."

"Hmmm," replied Zia. "I guess that could have worked." We walk comfortably, arm-in-arm, thinking about the Jonas Stockman story.

"Look, Aunt Zia. It's the cave. Let's go yell our names."

Zia and Ellen step over to the cave entrance. "You go first, Aunt Zia."

Zia bends into the cave entrance and shouts, "Ellen wins." The words reverberate back to Zia and Ellen, and they look at each other and laugh.

"Why did you say that, Aunt Zia?"

"Because, my girl, you are a winner. Always will be."

"I love you, Aunt Zia."

We walk the rest of the way in silence and stand side-by-side at the grave of Jonas Stockman. I lean over and brush leaves off the mound at the base of the tombstone. The top of the tombstone is crowded with the rocks we've left to show we care.

Zia leans the live cedar wreath up against the tombstone and says, "Here's to you, Revolutionary War Soldier Jonas Stockman. Merry Christmas!"

I echo, "Amen."

On the walk back through the woods, I catch her up on all that's happened in Marshall and in Callander. I remind her about Neta, and I tell her about going to see Mr. Wilson at the school board office.

"Aunt Zia, if Neta is nominated, I don't think that Mr. Wilson will send her picture to *The Mobile Press-Register*."

Aunt Zia is silent for a while then she says, "Ellen, one of my best friends is Sally Turner. Remember she works at *The Mobile Press-Register*? When the pictures are sent to be judged, call her. See if Neta's pictured is included. I'll write her to let her know that you'll be calling."

I thank Aunt Zia and move on to other topics. I tell her about talking to Aunt Eleanor about Ann Carson and reading the archived papers at the *Times-Standard*. Then we talk national news. She fears what is to come in Cuba and does not think that Batista can stay in power through the upcoming year. Cubans know how democracy works because the United States is so heavily involved in Cuba. Cubans, especially the upper class, know that democracy is so much more than they currently have under Batista.

Cuba seems a world away this Christmas.

Chapter Five: January 1959

Zia was closer than she could have guessed about the situation in Cuba. Batista left the country on New Year's Day. Castro took over immediately. People in the upper class of Cuba despise Batista and were excited about Castro taking over the country. They thought he would bring democracy with him. On the day that Castro, wearing his green army fatigues, rolls into Havana riding on a tank, the people line the street to welcome him. They wear the red and black of Castro's rebels and throw red carnations at his feet. Zia is there.

I'm in my bedroom listening to Buddy Holly's *Peggy Sue* when Dad yells up the stairs, "Time to go to Marshall." I turn off *Peggy Sue* and bounce down the stairs. I'm always ready to go to Marshall.

I slide into Dad's truck and glance over at him as he cranks the engine. He's dressed casually today. He fits together. . .worn shoes, old corduroy pants, flannel shirt. Comfortable is a great word to describe Dad. It also describes the way I feel around him, so comfortable I talk to him about the articles I've been reading at Lewis Henry's.

"I remember your mother talking about Ann; Ann was upset about something she found in President Hudson's office. Your mother didn't know what that *something* could be."

"There's just so much we don't know, Dad."

"Well, if you're bound and determined to pursue this, why don't you talk to your Granddaddy Callander about it?"

"Why Granddaddy?" I ask.

"Because he was one of five trustees at the college when your mother and Ann were there. He was appointed by the Governor and everything."

"I had no idea, Dad. You're right. He would be in a position to know the inner workings of the college. Thank you, Dad."

"You're welcome, sugar. Hope he helps you."

I turn on the radio and fiddle with the tuning knob until I get to the local station. *I Walk the Line* by Johnny Cash flows out of the radio. I lean back, close my eyes, and think about what Daddy just told me, and—I think about my mother.

I'm so angry at her right now. I'm angry she's dead. She won't be here for my prom or for my graduation. She won't be here when I leave for college. I can't even begin to consider that she may have left us on purpose.

When we get back from Marshall, I retreat to my room. It's my first chance to really study the book Aunt Zia gave me for Christmas. The book starts with some basic information on setting up interviews. Most of it is common sense, like making sure the person you are interviewing has a good solid base of information on the topic you are researching. I need to make sure the interviewee is a credible source.

"Once the interview is on the calendar, plan for the interview by preparing questions," I read. "Vary the types of questions that you plan to ask. Ask opening questions, factual questions, probe questions and throw in a hypothetical question."

I make lists of questions to ask David Henry Callander about his life, sorting them by question type:

✓ _Factual Questions_

1. How long has your family owned Callander?

2. Callander consists of how many acres?

3. How many tenants do you have?

✓ _Probe Questions_

1. Why is the plantation named Callander?

2. Explain how you acquired Callander.

3. How do the tenants earn their living?

✓ _Hypothetical Questions_

1. If you could live in any century, what century would you live in and why?

In reality, I'm going to talk to my grandfather about Marshall College, but writing this list of questions is good practice for when I'm in the field. Probe question: *Why do you think Neta Levy will not be the new Miss Marshall?* This is the question I most want to ask.

Monday is the day we nominate candidates for the Miss Marshall County High School Beauty Pageant. There is a special homeroom after second period so that classes can nominate their candidates. The senior class is meeting in the auditorium, and there is a lot of chatter as we pour into the room. We are given ballots as we enter the auditorium. Miss Taylor calls the meeting to order and opens the floor for nominations.

Mable's best friend stands up first and says, "I nominate Mable 'cause she'll be Miss Marshall. The senior class should have the winning candidate."

"Humph," says Liz.

Neta

I stand and nominate Neta Levy. Several other candidates are nominated before Miss Taylor closes the floor, and we write in our candidate on the ballot. I'm thankful I was not nominated. Miss Taylor thanks us for voting and dismisses us back to third period. On the way out, we stuff our ballots in the large brown box on the way out of the auditorium.

neta *

Class winners are announced over the intercom at the end of the day. I wait while the principal announces the freshman, sophomore, and junior winners. I hold my breath until I hear, "And the winner in the senior class is Neta Levy." I breathe.

Clubs meet after school to select their candidates, so I head to the *Voice* room after sixth period. Once again, Miss Taylor is in charge and opens the floor for nominations. Liz says, "I nominate Ellen Jones." She turns and looks at Mable saying, "*The Voice* wants to sponsor the winner."

I stand slowly. I knew this was coming, and I have strong feelings about the pageant because of Neta. It's a tough decision that will be impossible to explain. "Thank you so much for nominating me, but I've decided not to be in the pageant this year. I'm too busy right now." I add, "I nominate Liz Fuller." I sit down and turn to Liz, who is looking shocked. I don't want to tell her why I'm not going to be in the pageant.

Miss Taylor already knows. I can tell by her expression that she knows and she looks very sad.

Chapter Six: February 1959

I dread calling *The Mobile Press-Register.* I dial and hear the receptionist answer, "Mobile Press-Register. How may I direct your call?"

"May I speak to Miss Sally Turner, please?"

"Please hold while I transfer you." I hear the phone ringing and then, "Sally Turner. How may I help you?"

"Good morning, Miss Turner. It's Ellen, Zia's niece."

"Hi, Ellen. Zia wrote that you'd be calling."

"I'm sure you know why I'm calling. Is Neta Levy's picture one of the pictures sent from Marshall High School to be judged?"

"Hold the line, Ellen, and I'll go check."

I'm scared. Scared that Neta's picture will not be there. Scared that I'll get in trouble for calling.

"Ellen? You there?" questions Miss Turner.

"Yes, Miss Turner."

"Honey, I'm afraid there is no picture of Neta Levy. The pictures are alphabetized, and I've checked twice."

"Thank you so much for checking," I say. "I'll tell Aunt Zia that I talked to you."

I can sit here and stew, or I can do something productive. It's time to talk to my grandfather about his tenure as a Marshall College trustee. I want to know about 1938 and what Ann

Carson could have found in the president's office.

On the way to the plantation house, I pass by several tenants' homes. They look like houses on stilts. I think maybe they will begin to walk, crossing the adjoining fields in long strides. I laugh at the image.

Dogs are curled up under the clapboard houses for warmth. Spring is coming soon, but it's still chilly. The houses are constructed of wide, unpainted planks. Their front porches are filled with ladder-back chairs with sunken cane bottoms that sag halfway to the floor. Most tenant houses have three rooms, and each room has a roughly built, stone fireplace as its only means of heat. The yards are swept clean. There's not a blade of grass or a piece of trash to be seen. The last house in the row is Jo Jo's. His mother is on the porch, and I wave.

I walk across the long porch at the plantation house, enter the eight-foot doors, and turn left into my grandfather's study. I love to just stand and look at this room. The study is lined with bookcases on three walls. Some sections have books stored behind glass doors.

Grandfather is obviously not acquainted with the Dewey Decimal System. Books cover all the shelves haphazardly. I see Walt Whitman's *Leaves of Grass* next to Gibbon's *The History of Rome*. I see tons of books on law and engineering. I see ten years of *The Farmer's Almanac*. In the center of the room is a huge desk made of mahogany. The desk has a wide kneehole. I remember it was a perfect place for hiding when I was a child.

Grandfather is seated behind the desk and is tipped back in his high-backed, tufted leather chair. "Well, Ellen Jones. To what do I owe this honor? Come in, come in." He loves me dearly. This much I can tell.

I take a seat in the huge, overstuffed chair facing his desk and catch him up on my life. I do not mention Neta Levy, but I do tell him about finding out that Ann Carson and my mother were college roommates. I tell him about my visits to Lewis Henry's archives.

"Dad told me that you were a trustee at Marshall when mother and Ann were there," I say. "He said Ann found something in the president's office that upset her. Do you know what that might have been?"

"Well. . ." he replies. "I haven't thought of that time in years. It's been a pleasure to forget it entirely."

"Why's that, Grandfather?" I ask.

"We had to fire President Hudson two months after the SACS visit. We found he had falsified scores of students' achievement at the end of the course of studies in mathematics, biology, and chemistry. He also falsified the records of standardized tests scores. I personally had to contact the Southern Association of Colleges and Schools and provide them with this information. Marshall College was placed on sanctions for five years. It was a terrible time in the history of the town and the college. It would be my bet that Ann Carson realized these scores were inaccurate, and she died for it."

We sit in silence while I take in the implications of what he said. President Hudson, or someone, killed Ann Carson to save his own neck. As I get up to leave, my grandfather says, "Ellen, you need to know this has nothing to do with your mother."

I tell Dad and Aunt Essie about my conversation with Grandfather. Aunt Essie is surprised; Dad is not. The Marshall College situation was not discussed at the time it happened. If conversations occurred, they were in the privacy of kitchens or front parlors with the doors firmly closed. It was not publicized that President Hudson was fired. Or that he cheated, or that the college was on sanctions, or even that he was a murderer. Somehow, back then, protecting the reputation of the college was more important than publishing the truth. Though some townspeople had to know, most did not.

Aunt Essie quotes a verse, "Save me, Lord, from lying lips and from deceitful tongues. Psalm 120: 2."

Our conversation moves away from Marshall College, and now we talk about Cuba. Just months after he marched into power in those green fatigues, Castro took control of the Cuban government's 30,000-man army and was sworn in as prime minister on February 16, 1959. His brother, Raul Castro, performs mass executions of captured military. As many as five hundred Batista men have been executed. *Paredón* is a word heard on the streets of Cuba. Literally translated, it means "to the wall." In other words: "death by firing squad."

The executions are televised.

Dad has been able to talk to Zia via telephone. She, David, and the children are fine, but their life has been radically altered. Castro has taken away all David's ingenios. David received a letter from the president of Cuba thanking him for *donating* his ingenios to the Cuban government.

Castro pays David a salary and has allowed him to keep the Havana house. This is unusual because Castro has taken over the large homes left by the upper-class families leaving Cuba in droves. David can't think of leaving. He has progressive ideas about the sugar cane industry in his country and how to modernize it. David thinks Castro needs him.

Carlota and Julio still go to school and church. The militia, formed from former sugar cane workers, are everywhere. Castro brought them out of the fields to Havana and gave them guns. These militiamen line the sidewalk coming out of the Catholic

Church. When David, Zia, and the children, along with the rest of the congregation, walk out of the church, the militiamen spit upon them and call them names. I wonder how long Zia and David can remain in Cuba—this worries me.

Cuba and Marshall College are put on the back burner as I prepare for the next big event in my life—this year's senior play. _The Chaperone_ is about a senior class that takes a trip to New York City—except—the chaperone doesn't chaperone. Hair-raising encounters occur as the students make their way around The Big Apple.

Tryouts are after school today. I am trying out for the female lead along with Mable Johnson and half of the girls in the senior class. It's a big deal to have the lead.

Mrs. Thomas, the drama teacher, shouts to be heard over all the seniors crowded into the theater. "Thank you for coming in for tryouts this afternoon. Please be seated in the orchestra seats." She smiles when she says this. I get it. I smile back. Like we have a loge and orchestra seats in the theater at Marshall High!

I sit down with Liz, and she squeezes my hand, knowing that I'm nervous. "We are starting with tryouts for the lead. Mable, you'll be first."

Mrs. Thomas sits and waits for Mable to walk up the side steps to the stage. Mable parades to center stage, pauses, and begins.

While Mable is auditioning, I focus on some vocal exercises and whisper tongue twisters. "Betty Bramble bumbles through the bakery bins." Mable must have been pretty good because all the other seniors applaud as she exits the stage.

"Ellen Jones, you're next." I casually walk up the steps to

downstage right. I wait until I have Mrs. Thomas's full attention, and we make eye contact. I begin my monologue. "My heart beats out of my chest; it's trying to do that very thing. I cower as Sheila approaches and stands in front of me…"

I finish and take a small bow. "Thank you, Mrs. Thomas." I leave the stage. The cast will be announced tomorrow, and I am clueless as to how I performed.

The next morning, I dress with care. I put on my best school dress with a starched slip underneath. I brush my hair until it shines and put on a light smear of lipstick. I make sure my purse matches my shoes, and I leave. I can hardly wait to get there. The cast will be posted on the auditorium door.

When I arrive at the auditorium, a bunch of seniors is hovering near the door, waiting for the cast to be announced. We get really quiet as Mrs. Thomas opens the theater door and joins us in the hall. She takes thumb tacks out of her pocket and tacks the list of characters on the door. Smiling widely at the group of seniors, she goes back into the theater.

I am at the back of the crowd that surges up to the theater door. "Oh, I'm the chaperone in the play. Unreal," says Candy Michaels.

I elbow my way up to the door as Mable Johnson turns to leave the group. When she passes me, she looks me in the eye and says, "Tough luck, Ellen. You didn't win this one. I did!" I edge my way to the door. Sure enough, Mable Johnson has the lead. I get a role in the play, but I'm just one of the girls in the class that goes to New York. I turn and make my way to class.

That afternoon I drag out the whole process of seeing Dad

and Aunt Essie and telling them about the play. When I come in the back door, I take the time to make sure my wool coat and scarf are hung evenly on the antique coat rack. I drag the ear muffs off my head and place them on the shelf about the hooks. Seeing my reflection in the oval mirror that's centered on the rack, I think *Buck up, Ellen. You look awful!*

I take my time walking to the kitchen where I know Dad and Essie will be having afternoon coffee. Before they can ask, I say, "Well, I'm in the play—just one of the girls in the senior class who goes to New York. Mable got the lead."

Essie says, "That's great news that you're in the play."

Dad adds, "That's right, Ellen girl. I hope I don't have to tell you to give this role your all."

I know, I know—Dad expects me to do my best. I think about taking the high road during all those afternoon practices with Mable. Gonna be tough, but of course he's right. Dad changes the subject by handing me a long, legal-sized envelope with the University of Columbus on the return label. I know what it is. It's finally here.

"Dad, I just can't open it. You do it. Just let me down easy if it's a rejection," I say.

Dad carefully opens the envelope, pulls out the enclosed letter and reads it. He looks up at me and drawls, "Well, child, I guess you are a Columbus Cougar."

Suddenly, the school play is not so important after all. I'm going to college, and I'm going to the one I have dreamed about. Dad stands up, grabs me, and whirls me around the kitchen. When he puts me down, I see Essie over Dad's shoulder. She's teary eyed, and she's sliding a tissue back in her apron pocket. How blessed I am to have these two, wonderful people to share

srief

my good news. But—I miss Mother.

After supper, I go to my bedroom. I need to have a talk with my mother. "Mom, you weren't here this afternoon to hear all the news. I've got a minor role in the school play. Do you know that, up in heaven?" I pause and wait—waiting for an answer, I guess. "Mom, I'm going to Columbus University—it's where I really wanted to go, Mom. I'm going to study broadcast journalism. One day I'll be tagging my own stories. *Ellen Jones, CBS News.*" I add, "Mom, I don't know how much you know, but maybe things will be better if I talk to you from now on."

Dealing with grief

I feel a little of the tightness releasing—the tightness that's been in my chest since Mother died. Guess what? I don't feel so angry either. Actually, I'm feeling really good about myself.

Things are moving fast. The next day at school, we vote for the winner of the Miss Marshall High School Beauty Pageant. We don't know who the finalists are until we receive a ballot as we file into the auditorium.

I take my ballot and find a seat by Jo Jo. I open the folded ballot and see that both Mable and Liz are among the finalists. Neta Levy isn't even on the ballot! I vote for Liz and fold my ballot. The new Miss Marshall will be announced at the pageant in March. I put my ballot in the ballot box and walk out with Jo Jo.

JoJo

He says, "Um, Ellen. You should be Miss Marshall. You're sure the prettiest." He gives my hand a squeeze then walks off.

Chapter Seven: March 1959

Something happens that jerks me away from high school life and forces me to remember my mother—forces me to question why she died at all. I've pulled down the boxes holding Mother's life: her marriage box, my baby box, and the box of her college memorabilia.

In the box of college things, I run across a picture that I had never noticed. No wonder I never noticed it. It is tucked between the backboard of the leather graduation holder and the college diploma itself. Just a tiny, white edge is showing, and I pull on it.

It's a picture of a man who looks older than Mother. On the back of the picture is written, *To the love of my life*. Something tells me not to show this picture to Dad and Aunt Essie. I'll have to think about whom I can let see the picture. I slide the picture back behind the diploma.

mystery man

It's the night of the Miss Marshall High School Beauty Pageant. Everyone I know is working on the pageant or is in the pageant. I have to go; I can't just sit at home.

The auditorium is crowded. I search for a place to sit and see Liz's mother with an empty seat beside her. Stepping over several laps and feet, I take a seat.

"Hi, Mrs. Fuller. May I sit with you?"

"Sure, Ellen. I'm so nervous. I've bitten my nails to the quick. Be good to have you with me!"

I take her right hand in both mine and squeeze. "Don't you

worry, Mrs. Fuller. Liz is a winner!"

The pageant starts with the evening gown revue. *A Lovely Girl is Like a Melody* plays as Mable walks across the stage first. She's wearing black from head to toe. Her gown has a tight bodice with spaghetti straps, and the skirt is made of tons of organza. She's wearing high heels and totters just a little when she reaches mid-stage.

Liz is next. What a contrast! Liz is wearing a white, strapless gown that falls to the floor in simple, straight lines. Her shoes are white satin flats. She reaches mid-stage, faces the audience, and smiles a thousand-watt smile.

Next, the finalists perform a talent. There's baton twirling, poetry recitation, and dancing. Liz sings *Ole Man River*. It's an odd choice for a beauty pageant, but the poignant strands hang in the air long after the song is finished.

After speeches from the mayor and last year's Miss Marshall, the principal walks on the stage to announce the winner.

Liz Fuller! Mable takes second place.

I grab Miss Fuller's hand and say, "See Mrs. Fuller. I told you Liz is a winner."

I wish Aunt Zia were here. I'd love to tell her face-to-face about Miss Marshall and talk to her in person about heading off to college. Actually, I think I'd show her the picture I found in Mother's things first.

Aunt Zia, however, is not in a good place. Fidel Castro has nationalized not just the sugar cane industry but all the other industries as well. He has closed the Catholic churches and schools and even begun to send children to the Soviet Union to study on collective farms. Parents fear for their children in a communist society.

For now, Aunt Zia, David, and the children live in Havana. David works in the sugar cane industry for Fidel Castro, and Aunt Zia tries to make life as normal as possible for Carlota and Julio. Aunt Zia and the children have written me notes about my acceptance to the University of Columbus. She is so excited for me.

Saturday morning comes, bright and shiny. Dad, Aunt Essie, and I talk about the doings with some of the Callander tenants and everything left to do before graduation

After breakfast, I run up to my bedroom and slide the picture of the man found in Mother's college things between my blouse and skin. I've made a decision so I head for Aunt Eleanor's.

I find Aunt Eleanor arranging roses in the front parlor of the president's home. She's humming as she works. As always, she is immaculate in her long skirt and silk blouse. She turns and smiles as she sees me in the doorway.

"Oh, Ellen, you must come and have lemonade with me on the porch."

I follow her to the kitchen where she takes the heavy, glass pitcher out of the refrigerator. She's had this pitcher as long as I can remember and, in the spring and summer, it's always filled with fresh lemonade. We settle into the large rocking chairs on the porch and talk about spring at Marshall College and my going to the University of Columbus. We talk about how thrilled and sad my mother would be about my leaving home.

I finally get up the courage to pull the picture out of the front of my blouse. I hand it to Aunt Eleanor and say, "I found this picture hidden away in Mother's college things. It has an inscription on the back. Do you know who this man is, Aunt Eleanor?"

Aunt Eleanor blanches. She sits there for a long time, rocking, and clutching the picture to her chest.

"Aunt Eleanor, are you OK?" I ask. I'm very concerned that she's not OK at all. I can't imagine what has upset her so much. It must be the man in the picture. I wait for her to speak again.

Finally she says, "Oh, Ellen. You know the easy way to deal with the hard things in life is to shut them away in tiny compartments, seal them real tight, and hope that you never have to open those compartments again. This man has been stowed away in one of those compartments."

"His name was Ron Hester," she continues. "He came to Marshall in the early thirties and opened a bookstore. Your mother loved books, and she was always in that bookstore. One thing led to another, and she fell in love with him. As far as I know, I'm the only one who knew. Ann Carson was much too conservative to approve. Not that I did."

"What was wrong with that, Aunt Eleanor?" I ask. "He was obviously older than Mother, but that's not a sin. I know that she didn't meet Dad until after she had graduated and was working at Marshall College, anyway. What was the problem?"

"Oh, Ellen. He was married—and he had a young child," says Aunt Eleanor.

It's my turn to turn pale and stop rocking. I'm shocked to my core!

You know how those huge butterflies rumble in your stomach? You know how it feels when you hear something that you want to deny? You want to push it in one of Aunt Eleanor's tiny compartments and crawl in after it. That's how I feel, but there's more, and I can feel that whatever Aunt Eleanor is about to tell me is much worse than that.

"Ellen, I've watched you and Will struggle with your mother's death. The questions about suicide and not knowing must have been horrible. No wonder you haven't moved on yet and accepted her death. I can only tell you that there's more to the Ann Carson murder than anyone knows."

She looks me over then continues.

"Your mother could have saved John Maben's life and didn't. You see, she had already left campus on the night of the murder. She sneaked to the bookstore and met Ron. She was supposed to be back on campus by nine that night, but she didn't make it back until almost ten."

"As she walked in front of faculty housing on Marshall College campus, she saw John Maben and his wife, Deborah, sitting in their living room. They did not see her. Your mother could have testified that she saw John Maben at ten o'clock and backed up Deborah Maben's testimony. She knew if she did speak up, she would likely never graduate from Marshall, and she would most certainly have been shunned by the community if the story of where she'd been had come out, so Charlene chose to protect herself."

Aunt Eleanor looked at me, and when my eyes begged more, she went on. "She never saw Ron Hester again. She finished her degree and began working at Marshall College. She met your dad, and the rest is history. Can I judge her? No. I'm just as guilty. I was the only person who knew her story, and I kept quiet as well."

Truth and honor. I think of it again. I feel dirty and ashamed. I'm the child of a woman who let a man go to prison because she did not do the honorable thing and tell the truth. It doesn't matter that no one knows. I know. I have no doubt that, when Mother heard about John Maben's death in prison, she ran her car off that bridge. Evidently, she couldn't live with herself when he died in prison.

Truth +
Honor

How am I supposed to live with this? I believe human life is sacred. My own mother's lack of honor caused an innocent man to die in prison. She's gone, and she has left me with the weight of her terrible selfishness. In the hours that follow, I can barely function. All I can think about is John Maben and how my mother could have saved him.

Thank goodness the senior play is this weekend. I have practice every day after school. It will keep me occupied. I am not at home that much, so Dad and Aunt Essie can't sense my mood. The flip side of this is that I get to practice for hours and watch Mable Johnson in the lead. I renew my vow to take the high road.

Weeks pass. The play goes well. We even receive a standing ovation from the audience. To give Mable credit, she was pretty good in the lead role. Dad and Aunt Essie send me flowers backstage. I love that they did this and feel guilty because I'm keeping Mother's secret from them. I would probably tell Aunt Zia if she were here.

Cuba

I pray for Aunt Zia, Uncle David, and the children daily. News has filtered back to us that when Batista's followers were rounded up and killed in January and February, some United States citizens were killed as well. Were it not for the skill and innovative techniques that Uncle David brings to the sugar cane industry, we would be even more terrified for Aunt Zia. We have to trust that God will keep her safe and that, because of David's standing with Castro, they will not be harmed.

Monday after the play, during Mrs. Ander's English class, I look up to see Miss Taylor and the principal come in the classroom. They ask Mrs. Anders if they can see me in the hall. Mrs. Anders calls me to the front of the classroom and tells me to go out in the hall. *I'm terrified!* I've been carrying this awful secret inside me for weeks. This secret makes me feel inferior to just about everyone, even Mable Johnson. I'm worried the whole world knows about my Mother.

But wait. *Did I hear it right?* The principal is telling me I'm valedictorian of the Class of 1959. I have the highest grade point average in my class and will be the final speaker at graduation saying farewell to my classmates and teachers. What an amazing honor!

Vale,

Honor

I'm so excited about telling Aunt Essie and Dad. Can't imagine anything groovier. I am anxious to tell them over supper—but I wait. Dad says the blessing, "Bless this food to the nourishment of our bodies. Amen."

I wait. Essie picks up the cube steak topped with gravy and passes the dish to Dad. I start the bowl of pole beans, frozen from this past summer's garden and delicious during the winter. Finally, I say, "Miss Taylor and the principal pulled me out of English class today."

"Why ever on earth?"asks Essie, who paused to look at me while dishing up the beans.

"They wanted to tell me that I'm the valedictorian of the Class of 1959."

I drop the news just like that. Silence for a moment, then Dad gets up out of his chair and pulls me out of mine. He hugs me and cries. I have never seen my dad cry. Not even when Mother was buried.

Tears

Aunt Essie says, "The report I heard in my own country about your achievements and your wisdom is true. 2 Chronicles 9:5."

Chapter Eight: April 1959

The next afternoon I walk to the grave of Jonas Stockman and carry a branch from the tea olive tree to put on his grave. The tea olive is my favorite tree. Its smell is so sweet and exotic—it's almost like you can spoon the fragrance up, swallow it, and let it run down your throat. I stand at the grave and place the tea olive branch upon it.

Oh, help me Jonas. Am I a part of my mother? Am I less a person because I'm her child? Am I worthy to be valedictorian of my class?

[handwritten: Honor]

[handwritten: Sins of mother]

I tell Jonas about my mother and Ron Hester. Talking to Jonas makes the truth plain to me: I need to tell my father about Ron. I lay a small stone on the headstone of Jonas Stockman's grave and tell him that I'll see him later. I'm trudging home through the fields when I spot Jo Jo in the distance.

"Hey, Jo Jo Reed! What ya doing?"

"Lookin' for you."

"What's happening?"

He waits until he is closer to answer. I can't help but notice that his brown eyes are beautiful with the sunlight bouncing off them. Oh my, there's that dimple that shows when he smiles, and that flutter I keep feeling around Jo Jo.

[handwritten: Prom]

"Well, you know that prom is coming up the end of the month. I'd like you to go to prom with me, Ellen."

Prom? I'd forgotten about prom. Where's my head? My heart pounds in my chest at the thought of going to prom with Jo Jo.

Of course, I want to go to prom my senior year. Of course I want to go with Jo Jo.

"Jo Jo Reed," I say, "I'd love to go to prom with you."

He slowly reaches over, lifts my chin, and lowers his lips to mine. We stand in that field a long time, holding on to that kiss. When we break apart, he seems embarrassed.

"Hmmm. Well, Ellen. I'll see you later." Jo Jo turns and walks away.

I stand watching him until he disappears from sight. *Gosh, I'm going to prom with Jo Jo! Even better, Jo Jo just kissed me. Life can be good.*

But life doesn't feel so good this morning. It's Saturday morning, and this is the morning that I'm gonna tell Dad about Ron Hester. After breakfast, I tell Aunt Essie to go ahead with her visits to the tenants' houses. "I'll do the breakfast dishes, Aunt Essie," I say.

When she leaves, I try to tell Dad about Ron Hester and the whole story about Mother being off campus the night of Ann Carson's murder. I try, but I'm crying—crying so hard I can hardly talk.

Dad sits down in the chair across from me and drags it forward until he's directly in front of me. He takes both my hands in his. "Ellen, what's wrong, girl?"

I shake my head to tell him I can't talk.

"Take your time. I'll be right here. When you can, you tell me what's so awful."

My dad is a patient man. He just sits there, waiting until I can talk.

When I finally do talk, I blurt it all out. I can't get it out fast enough. Mother was off campus the night of Ann's murder. She saw John Maben and his wife as she was coming back to her dorm. Mother did not testify for John. I think Mother committed suicide because she felt so guilty. And I feel some responsibility—I'm her daughter."

Dad listens. He is sitting on the edge of his chair, hunched over with elbows on his knees and his hands squeezed together. He's looking at the floor. I wait. Finally, Dad lifts his head and looks me in the eye.

"Ellen, I keep seeing your mother as I saw her for the first time. I had come to see David Henry about his cotton crop. Your mother and Eleanor were sitting on the front porch of the plantation house—that same porch that you love to hang out on. Your mother was so sassy, asking, 'And who would you be?' as I came up the steps. I looked in those blue eyes surrounded by all that blonde hair, and I fell—fell hard. I never dated another girl from that moment on."

"Don't think your mother dated anyone else either," he said. "That woman loved taking care of people. She sure took care of me—and you, when you came along a few years later. Sometimes she'd go into herself. We couldn't follow when she did that. I never knew what she thought about then. Maybe John Maben. . ."

"Dad, do you think she committed suicide?"

He takes his time. "We'll never be able to prove it, Ellen, but I suppose it wouldn't surprise me. Imagine your mother living with what she did all those years." Dad adds, "Ellen, your mother was so young when all this happened. She was young, and she was in love."

"But Dad, how could she let an innocent man go to prison?"

mistakes of youth

Dad answers, "Again, she was young and, I imagine, scared to death. We have to try not to judge her. I know how hard that is. You must know that she loved us deeply. She was so proud of you. She was a wonderful wife and mother. I will miss her every moment of every day forever." With that, he gets up out of his chair, leans over, and kisses me on the top of my head.

Dad sits back down again. I expect to feel better for sharing Mother's story, but I don't. I feel the same. We just sit there in silence. After a long time, Dad says, "Come on, it's time to go into town."

Of course, we go into Marshall. It's Saturday. One of my favorite things to do is visit Lewis Henry on Saturday, and naturally I head for *The Marshall Times-Standard* building. Mr. Henry is in top form when I walk in.

"Ellen, come sit. Come sit."

I crawl up on the rickety stool at his workbench and take the pictures that he offers. "Let's talk about angles. Look at this wonderful shot from my Scotland trip. This is Edinburgh Castle, and I'm standing on the sidewalk below the castle. A low angle is used in this shot. This shot involves the placement of the camera below the subject. The camera is shooting up. This makes the subject appear large and powerful."

"I see that, Mr. Henry. Really makes a difference," says Ellen.

"Straight angles involve the viewer. The subject in the shot is looking directly into the camera lens, and the camera is placed at eye level. When you watch Chet Huntley and David Brinkley, notice that the angle of the shot is straight. We feel that the newscasters are talking directly to us. Shots would be pretty boring if we only shoot straight angles. When you shoot a subject, get above it. Get below it. Shoot it straight on and shoot it from the side. Print your pictures and see the difference. Life's

Photos

View point

like that, too. You have to look at it from different perspectives."

I think Lewis Henry is on to something there. Maybe there's a different angle to consider with all that happened years ago.

When I get home Essie is yelling, "Hurry Ellen. It's a letter to you from Zia. The postman just delivered it."

I take the letter and open it. A note and a check are inside. Zia has written—

—Even though I can't be there with you for your first prom, I still want to be a part of it. Take this check and go to Gayfer's in Mobile. Buy yourself the most stunning prom dress you can find. Buy some shoes to go with it.

All my love,

Zia

The next Saturday, Dad, Essie, Liz, and I load into the car to go to Gayfer's in Mobile. On the way, Liz shows me her slam book. The heading of a page at the back of the book is, *Who in our class will win a Pulitzer Prize?* Beside every number on the page is my name, *Ellen Jones*.

Me? A Pulitzer Prize? I feel tears welling in my eyes. Imagine my classmates thinking so highly of me.

Liz and I talk about next year. "Liz," I say, "I know you want to go to Marshall College, but I wish you were going to Columbus University with me."

"Aw, Ellen, look at it this way. I'll be here to fill you in on all the goings-on in Marshall. Did you know that ole Mable is going to Marshall, too? Can't get away from Dad!"

"Poor you! Liz, do you want to stay in Marshall all your life?"

Liz
Dreams

"There are worst things. Besides, I think that I want to teach high school English. I can do that anywhere."

"You're my best friend for life, Liz. I'll miss you terribly next year. Now help me pick out a totally cool prom dress!" The first dress that I spot in the teens' department at Gayfer's is the one. I know it right away. It's so feminine. The top is ruched or gathered and falls softly off the shoulders. It's baby pink chiffon with a twirling full skirt. There's a satin layer to the skirt topped with two layers of chiffon. I try it on; it's perfect. I feel like I'm floating.

Next, I buy pink satin, open-toed shoes that have a rhinestone pin on the top. The shoes have a small heel. Maybe I can handle these, I think. Can't forget hose. I buy seamed neutral hose—I will just have to work on keeping the seams straight. I get a pink garter belt to go with the hose. For one night, I'll be Ellen Jones, totally stunning girl. Maybe. Zia will be proud of me.

We can't leave Mobile without eating at Wintzell's on Dauphin Street. Dad loves oysters, and he starts salivating when he sees the sign: *Wintzell's. Oysters. Fried, Stewed or Nude.* I settle for fried shrimp, slaw, and the best hushpuppies in Alabama. Humph! Better watch it or I won't fit in my prom dress.

Jo Jo and I walk into the prom arm in arm. The gym is decorated with gauzy material floating from the ceiling in waves. Caught up in the material are hundreds of stars. The prom night theme is *Stars Fell on Alabama.*

Jo Jo and I dance for the first time to *In the Still of the Night* by the Five Satins. I look around at all my classmates and teachers and feel the deepest love. All Alabama stars! We bop to *Great Balls of Fire* by Jerry Lee Lewis and *At the Hop* by Danny and the Juniors. Miss Taylor steals the show when she and Coach Moore dance to *Little Darlin'* by the Diamonds.

Jo Jo and I walk outside to the front steps of the gym. We lean against the tall columns on the porch and talk about school, about Marshall, and about leaving Marshall.

Jo Jo says, "Ellen, I've got some news. Only my parents know. I wanted to tell you first before I tell anyone else."

"Well, come on, Jo Jo. Don't keep me in suspense."

"I'm going to the Air Force Academy."

"That's great, Jo Jo—where is it?"

"In Colorado, near Colorado Springs. I want to be in the Air Force and want to go in as an officer for sure. Actually, I'll go in as a second lieutenant."

"I didn't know. I didn't know you wanted to be in the military, but I can sure see you as an officer. Isn't it hard to get in any of the academies?"

"Yeah! Pretty hard. I had to get a congressional nomination from Senator Hill before I could apply. You know there are only so many nominated each year so I feel pretty lucky."

"Oh poo, Jo Jo! You're a shoo-in for any college or academy. They'll be lucky to have you."

"Ellen, you know that I'm really gonna miss you. If I could have any girl, it would be you. You're not gonna go to that school in Miami and forget me, are ya?"

"Not likely I could forget you, Jo Jo. Not likely at all."

Chapter Nine: May 1959

You know, it's really funny how things work out. Sometimes help comes where you least expect it.

Dad left for work early this morning, and it's just Aunt Essie and me for breakfast. We're at the table together eating my favorite, bacon and French toast. Aunt Essie slowly swirls the syrup on her plate while I eat.

She finally puts down her fork, looks me in the eye, and says, "Ellen girl, you've got to let your mother go. We don't know about her death, and we probably never will. We all have to move on. You need to know that you are a shining child who will grow up and do wonderful things. You are not your mother."

She closes by saying, "The soul who sins is the one who will die. The son will not share the guilt of the father, nor will the father share the guilt of the son. Ezekiel 18:20."

It has been eight months. I cry—cry for my beloved mother, who, I'm pretty sure, felt she couldn't live any longer. I cry for Dad and for myself because we have to live without her.

As I write my valedictorian speech, I think of where I want to go in life—I look back too. I think of my parents, my three aunts, and all the good people who live at Callander. I think of the faculty at Marshall High School and members in the Class of 1959. In a way, it's just too sad. A little piece of each person is a part of who I am.

What can I give this life and nation knowing what I love to

do the most?

Dreams

I want to write. Write about hope—hope for our future. I finish my speech and get it approved by the senior advisors, Miss Rebecca and Mrs. Taylor.

Graduation night arrives and I stand to deliver my farewell to the class of 1959. I deliver my speech on hope, but I don't end there. I pull the dog-eared editorial about Neta Levy out from under my notes and read it to the audience. I conclude, "So, who is the fairest of them all? In my book, it's Neta Levy, and we should applaud her as a winner."

The Beauty

Silence.

I can hear my heart pounding as I wait for a reaction. Then—a spontaneous roar as the crowd comes to its feet and applauds for Neta Levy.

The beauty

Through all the noise, I recall Luella and her three predictions for me. Two predictions are yet to be fulfilled, but tonight I have been an advocate for the beauty of Neta Levy.

"Very good, Luella!" I say as I walk off the stage. "Very good, indeed."

Ellen's Notebook: 1958 – 1959

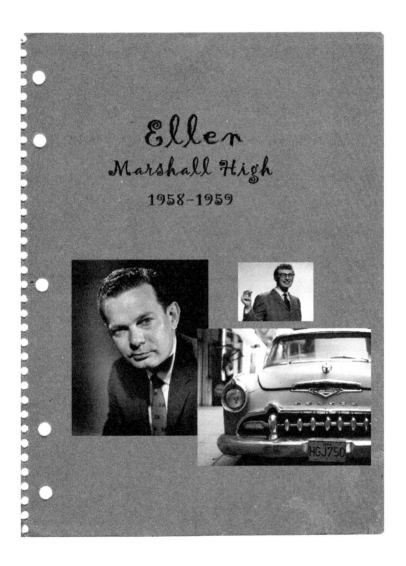

CAMERA SHOTS

The basic camera shots are: long shot, medium shot, close-up, and extreme close-up. It is important to use a variety of shots when telling a story.

Long Shot (LS)

A long shot shows the setting where the action is taking place. If a long shot is used at the beginning of a scene, it's often called an establishing shot.

This shot of Lewis Henry is a long shot. In the shot, we see that he is on a street in downtown Marshall.

Medium Shot (MS)

A medium shot cuts out most of the setting. The viewer is focused on the subject in a medium shot.

A medium shot of a person usually begins right above the top of the head and ends at the waist.

In this medium shot of Lewis Henry, it's important to show the newspaper in the shot. If you don't show the copy of the newspaper, the viewer doesn't understand why Mr. Henry is looking down.

Close-up (CU)

A close-up is used to show the most important part of the subject. If the subject is a person, a close-up would be of the head. Close-ups bring the viewer closer to the action.

Remember Lewis Henry talked about how important close-ups are.

Extreme Close-up (XCU)

An extreme close-up focuses on one detail. An XCU of a person could be the mouth or eyes. Extreme close-ups allow the viewer to see the emotions displayed on the subject's face.

CAMERA ANGLES

It's interesting to look at a subject from different perspectives. Try shooting a subject from these angles: straight, side, high, and low.

Straight Angle

Straight angles involve the viewer. The subject in the shot, the cow, is looking directly into the camera lens, and the camera is placed at eye level. When you watch Chet Huntley and David Brinkley, notice that angle of the shot is straight. We feel that they are talking directly to us.

Side Angle

Side angles find us, the viewer, looking on at an action that is occurring. The camera is placed at eye level, but it is placed at a 95-degree angle or more. The viewer is not involved in the action; the viewer is watching the action.

High Angle

High angles involve the camera placed above the subject; the camera is shooting down on the subject. This makes the subject appear smaller and less significant.

Low Angle

Low angles involve the camera placed below the subject. The camera is shooting up. This makes the subject appear larger and more powerful.

SCRIPTWRITING

This is what Aunt Zia taught me about writing hard news stories for broadcast news. A story has three parts—the lead, the body, and the conclusion.

The **LEAD** tells you who is involved in the story, what happened, where did it happen, and when did it happen. The lead may also tell you why it happened and how it happened.

The **BODY** gives you facts about the story and adds flesh to the story.

The **CONCLUSION** tells the viewer what comes next in the story, or it recaps the lead. Stories are written in a split-page format. Video is described on the left, and audio is written on the right.

VOs, SOTs and VO/SOTs

Aunt Zia: "Remember that the viewer is hearing and seeing the story. You have to plan and explain what the viewer is seeing."

VO stands for "voiceover" which means that you hear the reporter or anchor, but you see footage that supports what they are saying. In my first script, Zia is talking about the story of Terry Malloy, but we are seeing Marlon Brando at the docks.

SOT stands for "Sound on Tape"; it means a sound bite from a recording, such as an interview. There's a SOT in my first script; we see and hear Elia Kazan talking about the origins of "On the Waterfront".

SOTs need to be brief. You may start a portion of the script as an SOT, and then you add footage that compliments the SOT. That's a VO/SOT.

MY FIRST SCRIPT

"On the Waterfront"

CBS
Zia Jones
March 31, 1955

Suggested anchor lead-in:	It's almost a sweep! The Academy Awards were presented on March 30, 1955, at the RKO Pantages Theatre in Hollywood, and "On the Waterfront" was the big winner!
Scene from "On the Waterfront": (Marlon Brando with Eva Maria Saint)	VO---"On the Waterfront" won best picture, and its director, Elia Kazan, won the best director award. Marlon Brandon won the best actor award and Eva Maria Saint won as best supporting actress.
Scene from "On the Waterfront": (Marlon Brando at the docks)	VO---"On the Waterfront" is the story of Terry Malloy, a dockworker, whose brother is affiliated with a mob boss. The setting is the docks of Hoboken, New Jersey. Terry is instrumental in the murder of a popular dockworker by coaxing him into an ambush. Terry is conflicted; he wants to testify against the boss.

Elia Kazan, director: "On the Waterfront"	SOT---Elia Kazan "ON THE WATERFRONT" WAS BASED ON A 24-PART SERIES OF ARTICLES PRINTED IN THE NEW YORK SUN THAT COVERED RACKETEERING ON THE WATERFRONTS OF MANHATTAN AND BROOKLYN. THE SERIES WON THE 1949 PULITZER PRIZE FOR LOCAL REPORTING.
Shot of Eliz Kazan directing a scene from "On the Waterfront":	VO---The next film on the horizon for Elia Kazan is "East of Eden".
Zia Jones CBS Evening News	Once again, the big winner at the academy awards is "On the Waterfront".

TYPES OF NEWS STORIES

A **HARD news story** is a factual accounting of a current event. Factual stories of breaking events, such as earthquakes or the election of Eisenhower, are hard news stories.

A **SOFT news story** is usually not time sensitive. Profiles of people are categorized as soft news stories. A soft news story may entertain.

An **EDITORIAL** is written from a personal point of view. Editorials express the opinion of the writer. Opinions are forbidden in other types of stories.

INTERVIEWING

Know why you are interviewing this person. To consider: Is this person a reliable source for the story? If you are writing a hard news story about the anniversary of D-Day ideally you will want to interview a soldier that was involved in the invasion. Interviewing a person who has seen all the war movies about D-Day is not the same thing.

Research

Do your research to learn information about your subject before the scheduled interview. What is their background? How are they tied in to your story and why? This will help you plan questions. Plan a variety of questions for the person that you are interviewing. Ask factual questions that are short-answer questions about the person and their experience with the subject that you are researching. Example: How old were you when you joined the Army?

Probe questions

Ask more probe questions. These require longer answers. Example: Why did you join the Army? Don't forget to get the interviewee to expand their answers. Asking why and how will do that.

Hypothetical questions

Ask a **hypothetical** question. Hypothetical questions allow you to find out things about the subject that you might not know otherwise. Example: If you could be any general during WWII, who would you be and why?

Arrive early

It's important that you <u>arrive early</u> to the interview. You have to allow the cameraman time to set up the tripod and camera and to mic the subject. While this is happening, make friendly conversation with the subject. This helps the subject relax.

List of questions

Once the camera is rolling and the interview has begun, you are ready with your <u>list of questions</u>. The worst thing that you can do is to go down the list in order and never respond to what the interviewee says or ask him to expand or explain a certain fact. If he tells you that he's related to General Patton, you are not going to ignore this fact and keep on with your list of questions. You want to know about this relationship. Ask questions!

Thank the subject

Once the interview is over, <u>thank the subject</u> and offer to send them a copy of your hard news story after it has aired. This is a gracious way to thank the interviewee for his time.

Part Two: Ellen and the Dictator

Chapter Ten: September 1960

It's 9:00 p.m., and I'm cramming for a calculus exam. Calculus is my nemesis. The telephone down the hall starts to ring, interrupting my thoughts of an integral's function. I'm in Caldwell Hall, an underclassmen's dorm at Columbus University in Miami, Florida. Phones are located in wooden telephone booths on each floor of the old dorm. I hear, "Ellen Jones. Call's for you."

I plop down in the old booth. "Ellen Jones here. . ."

"Hi there, Ellen. It's your father."

"Hi, Dad. Everything good at Callander?"

"Sure, sure. Everything's fine. Listen Ellen, I need to talk to you about Zia and the family. Things have gotten so bad in Cuba that David plans to send Julio to the United States."

"Things are really that bad?"

"Zia says they are. They are surrounded by people who snitch. If anyone in the family makes a negative comment about the state of affairs in Cuba, a neighbor or friend may tell someone in the government. The government punishes those who speak out against what's happening in any number of ways, none pleasant. And then there's this business of the children studying Marxism in school. They want Julio out of Cuba right now."

Cuba under Castro

"Is that gonna be hard to do?"

"Probably so, but there's just no other way. Zia says a secret organization is helping parents send their children to the United States. David will have to get Julio a visa from the American

Embassy. Here's where you come in—you have to pick up Julio at the Miami airport. We're all counting on you, Ellen. Will you do it?"

"Of course. I'll be there. Dad, I just hate this for Zia—for all of them."

"Me, too. I'll stay in touch, and we'll talk more about the details. Remember, I'm coming to campus for your birthday."

My birthday. I had almost forgotten it, my head is so full of functions at the moment.

The next day, after taking the dreaded calculus exam, I head for my favorite part of campus, the broadcasting studio. The journalism school, or J-school for short, is located in the middle of the campus, and what a beautiful, historic campus it is. Although so many of the older buildings on campus are Greek Revival style with tall, rounded columns, the J-school is very modern. The front of the building is three floors of curved glass.

Broadcast Journalism is on the third floor, and the studio is positioned so that the main set is in front of all that glass. The audience sees the campus behind the anchors on the set on our daily show. I've hung out so much in the department they let me sit in on meetings, and sometimes I even run a camera during the show.

dreams

Today is such a day. Dr. Shelby runs the department and teaches the advanced classes. When I walk in the studio, he yells, "Ellen, you're on camera two. Get your headset on."

I stand behind the studio camera and take hold of the two handles on each side of the camera. The rough leather feels natural in my hands. I zoom all the way in on the logo that's on the front of the anchor desk and focus on the cougar with *Miami News Now* written below in navy blue letters. I zoom out again.

Now the focus will hold throughout the show, no matter what type of shot I have to get. I open the piece with a two-shot. That means both news anchors will appear in my shot. Later in the show, I'll get a medium shot of one of the two anchors. In the medium shot, the audience will see the anchor from the waist up.

I hear, "Standby." The floor director's right hand goes high in the air with the palm facing outwards. He begins the countdown to air, "5—4—3." He never actually says the numbers two and one. His audio would be too close to air time and might be heard.

The anchors open with, "Good evening, and welcome to *Miami News Now.*"

I always get goose bumps up and down my arms when I hear the opening.

Cynthia Farmer and Luke O'Neal make a great team. Cynthia is a beautiful brunette with large green eyes. She's friendly and is open to answering my questions. Luke, on the other hand, is an egotistical jerk. His hair is dark and close-cropped with a square jaw. Drop-dead gorgeous. Too bad his personality doesn't match his face. He thinks he is so superior—calls himself "Luke the Legend" and calls me "Maid of Cotton."

I enjoy sticking around for Dr. Shelby's after-show critique. I especially like the fact that he chews Luke out for missing a floor director's cue. I am still replaying the shows in my head at the end of a long week, curled up in my bed and dreaming of the day I will be the anchor.

Ah, Saturday—my day to sleep in. Well, maybe not. Aunt Essie calls and interrupts my dreams of being on air at the CBS station in New York City. This morning she's really on a tear. She has breaking news: my father is seeing another lady.

"Her name is Amanda Weyland," she informs me. According

Religious Bias #

to Aunt Essie, <u>she's all wrong for my father because she's Presbyterian, not Methodist.</u>

"Charlene's only been dead two years," Essie says. "Why does he have to see anybody?"

I'm shocked at the news myself. Humph! I'll have to think about this.

Aunt Essie hangs up, but not before saying, "To keep thee from the evil woman, from the flattery of the tongue of a strange woman. Proverbs 6:24."

Chapter Eleven: October 1960

"Happy birthday to you. Happy birthday to you. Happy birthday, dear Ellen. Happy birthday to you!" That's my roommate singing. She sounds like a frog. She may not be able to sing, but she is a fabulous roommate. She's from Alabama, too, from Mobile, and she's a Spanish major.

She ends her song by shouting, "¡Feliz cumpleaños!"

It's the first of October, my birthday. Amanda and Dad are flying into Miami. They're going to spend some time with me and take me out to dinner. I don't know how to feel about this. I'm not sure that I'm ready for Amanda. You grow up with a mother and father, and you expect both of them to always be there. It's hard enough living without Mother. Replacing her seems impossible. Actually, it hurts. I don't want to think about this on my birthday. *Grief after death*

The dorm mother leans into my room to tell me Dad and Amanda are in the lobby. I'm glad I have that long walk down the hall and the stairs to compose myself. When I reach the bottom of the stairs, I see my Dad, who's wearing a sports coat and tie for the occasion. Standing beside him is this perfectly formed, petite blonde. She's about five-foot-five and is wearing a sleeveless, purple wool dress that is stunning. Her hair is in a French twist—not one hair out of place. My grandfather Callander would say she has great bone structure. To me, she looks expensive.

Dad grabs me and kisses me. "Happy birthday, girl," he says. "I've brought someone to meet you."

I shake Amanda's hand, feeling like Godzilla towering over all that exquisiteness.

I suggest we start off by walking across campus to the broadcasting studio. Dr. Shelby knows Dad and Amanda are coming. He has assured me that it's fine for them to stand in the studio and watch the show—then we enter into chaos. The lead story is not ready, and we go on air in five minutes. Cynthia and Luke are at the anchor's desk arguing about a news package at the end of the show.

Luke says, "Cynthia, you wouldn't know a good lead if it walked up and spat in your face. Who, what, where, and when, girl!" Luke is his usual know-it-all self. They only stop arguing to do sound checks.

Dr. Shelby, more frazzled than usual, yells for me to take camera two. I show Dad and Amanda where to stand and walk to camera two. It's funny—I put my headset on and that feeling of excitement is back. I forget everything else except running the camera.

Despite the chaos, the show is great. It usually is. I'm so glad Dad got to see the show. I introduce him to Dr. Shelby and while the two of them are talking, I take Amanda to meet Cynthia and Luke. It turns out Amanda took broadcast journalism classes at the University of Alabama and, at one time, wanted to be a reporter. I am surprised to see how easily she talks to Cynthia and Luke. Luke surprises me, too. For once, the words "Maid of Cotton" don't escape from his mouth.

Dad tells Dr. Shelby about how we watch the news every night at our house, like he wants Dr. Shelby to know what a wonderful prospective student I'll be. I interrupt his diatribe. "Thank you, Dr. Shelby, for letting Dad and Amanda watch. I'll see you tomorrow."

Outside Dad turns and says, "Ellen, Amanda has made reservations at a wonderful restaurant for your birthday dinner." I'm surprised. I had hoped we would ride out to the beach and get a Cuban sandwich with Tres Leches for dessert. I remain quiet on the way to the restaurant. Actually, I am sullen and silent.

The dinner is a flop. The restaurant is in Coral Gables. It has white tablecloths and a sommelier, for gosh sakes. Do they really need a wine professional? Conversation among Dad, Amanda, and me is stiff, to say the least. I talk to her about people in Marshall and during our conversation discover she is a widow. Her husband was Doctor Weyland, who came to Marshall after my pediatrician, Dr. Moore, passed away.

The dinner talk turns to Zia and David's resolution to get Julio out of Cuba. Dad says, "We have to help Julio. When and if he gets out of Cuba and comes to the United States, David wants Julio enrolled in a preparatory school. I've talked to some people, Ellen, but I'd like to see what you can come up with."

"Well, Dad. Let me put the campus library to use. I'll see what I can find."

Dad and Amanda's return flight to Birmingham takes off soon so we finish up our desserts; no Tres Leches for me tonight. As we walk out, I promise Dad to be in touch about the prep schools and thank him for coming to Miami to celebrate with me. I'm aware that Dad spent quite a bit of money flying down, but I'm still resentful. The drive back to my dorm is silent, and I can see that Dad is hurt. I'm hurt, too.

The next day I'm in the control room at the J-school. I am watching the CBS evening newscast on one of the many small monitors located in the rack above the control room desk. It's not loud enough, so I reach over to the audio board and slide the fader up for the monitor. One of the hard news stories is about the children in Cuba.

It seems David and Aunt Zia are right to try to get Julio to the United States. Some children are being sent to the Soviet

Cuba

Union to study on collective farms. For the first time, I imagine how desperate David and Aunt Zia must be. If the children aren't sent out of Cuba, they will be indoctrinated with communism. Castro has formed youth groups, so children of all ages will be taught the communist way. Parents who oppose their children's indoctrination are considered anti-revolutionary and are in danger.

It is rumored that Castro may abolish *Patria Potestad* or the legal rights of parents over their children. If that happens, the Cuban government can decide where each child will go to school, what they will study, and where they will live. David and Aunt Zia will have to be careful. I say a prayer for them. My thoughts turn to Julio. *Does he understand what's going on in his country?*

I also say a silly prayer that I won't make a fool of myself tonight. There's a street dance on campus, and Ann has been working with me all week. She's teaching me the Twist. I've tried to do the Twist to *Let's Twist Again Like We Did Last Summer* and *Twist and Shout* so many times by now I should be a pro, but I am a slow learner. Finally, Ann has to get down on the floor and move my knees to the music. *Hey! Now I get it! I'm twisting!*

These dances just spring up like they have a life of their own. The word will start spreading across campus, "Hey, we're dancing tonight." or "Wayne Moore is singing tonight." Wayne is a senior on campus who sounds just like Ray Charles. You can close your eyes when he sings *The Night Time is the Right Time* and swear you're hearing Ray Charles.

Ann and I, along with the other girls on our hall, get to the dance late, and Ann is immediately swept onto the dance floor. I stand back and watch her. She's so full of energy and joie de vive—all five-feet-five of her. What a picture she makes twirling around the floor with her skirt of blooming, red roses and a white peasant blouse tied at the neck. She's moving so fast her dishwater-blonde hair is standing straight out.

The next song calls for the twist. Oh, Lord! Luke from broadcasting is walking across the floor toward me. He says, "Come on, Maid of Cotton. Let's see what ya got." I want to turn around and run. I don't—instead, I take his hand and move onto the floor. I can do this. He starts twisting, and I follow. My arms are pumping parallel to the floor, and my knees move from side to side. I laugh out loud.

Who would have thought that I'd be twisting with Luke the Legend? I love this. The dance is over, and Luke says, "Thanks, Cotton. You're not half bad." You know, that man is really good-looking.

The day after the dance, I'm crossing campus, thinking about the dance. I turn in to the old brick campus post office and open my mail box. I rarely get mail because everyone, especially Dad, calls instead of writing. I am surprised to see two letters in the mailbox: one from Aunt Essie and the other is from Amanda.

Our campus is filled with huge trees with low-hanging limbs decorated with gray Spanish moss that droops in large, matted clusters. The trees remind me of the old crones' hair from my childhood picture books. I find a bench underneath one of the trees and prepare myself to read Essie's letter first. Can you say vitriol? Whew! It seems Amanda is moving into Essie's territory, and Essie is furious. She didn't withhold any of it in her letter.

Amanda has started eating with Dad and Essie on Sundays, insisting they eat in the dining room, not the kitchen. According to Essie, Amanda's setting the table with a white tablecloth and the family silver in the Old Master's pattern. Fresh flowers and greenery have to be set in the middle of the table, and all food dishes are placed on the dining table. Of course, they're served in the Syracuse china. Essie writes, "Ellen, you know that Will likes to eat. He doesn't like to dine, and we're dining."

She's right. When I was at home, we always served our plates from the kitchen stove, and ate at the kitchen table. Meals are my best time when visiting. We all share the day and enjoy Essie's food—especially her Country Captain, which she fixes most Sundays.

It seems Country Captain is not the fare anymore. Essie says they are eating lamb chops with something called balsamic reduction. As usual, Aunt Essie closes with a quote, "Give us today our daily bread. Mathew 6: 11."

Well, that was interesting. I prepare myself for Amanda's letter.

Despite the preparation, I am surprised. She begins by thanking me for allowing her to celebrate my birthday with Dad. It occurred to her that I might have wanted to choose the restaurant for my birthday. She's sorry if she made a mistake and just wanted me to be surprised and have a special dinner.

She goes on to say she really wants to talk with me about broadcasting and Aunt Zia's career. It seems she chose an early marriage over a career in journalism. I feel the slightest softening toward her and wonder about her previous marriage. Essie says Amanda's husband was loud and outgoing. What a contrast to my quiet, self-contained father.

She changes topics and tells me what a fine person my Dad is then, shock of all shocks, she admits being terrified of meeting me and spending an evening with my dad and me, especially one so important as my birthday. She adds that she raised two sons and has no idea how to relate to a daughter. *Wow! That took guts*, I think. I have to admit I'm impressed. She closes by saying Dad has news from Zia and will call one night this week.

On Friday night Dad calls. Big news. David has started the process for Julio to obtain a visa for entry into the United

Cuba
Children

States. David made contact with James Baker, who teaches at Reston Academy, an American school in Havana. Mr. Baker is instrumental in organizing a network to get children out of Havana.

"Baker is working with Father Bryan O. Walsh in Miami," Dad tells me. "Father Walsh is involved with the Catholic Social Service Agency. It's a secret organization David and Zia heard about." He tells me Baker helps the children get out of Cuba then Father Walsh makes sure they are taken care of once they reach Miami. While I'm still listening to Dad, I decide to visit Father Walsh.

I learn from Dad that most of the planning that occurs between James Baker and Father Walsh happens by letters exchanged back and forth through the *diplomatic pouch*, a sealed bag used by government leaders for the transport of classified material to their embassies located in other countries. It cannot be searched or taken.

Mr. Baker has instructed David to visit the U.S. Embassy where the process of getting a student visa for Julio has begun. David declares he is sending Julio to Alabama to spend Christmas with Will and Essie. The visa is approved, and Julio is to fly to the United States in December.

When I'm at Callander, there are lots of places for me to do what I call my soul-searching. I don't have a place for this at the university, so I go to the bench where I read the letters from Zia and Amanda. I process everything that has happened during the last two months and think about the path ahead.

It's easy to swear I'll help David, Zia, and Julio. The harder and much more personal decision involves Amanda. It will be hard to adjust to Dad's being with someone other than my mother. She might be OK. We'll see.

Chapter Twelve: November 1960

It's a beautiful Saturday morning on the University of Columbus campus, and the old, stately library is waiting. I'm on a mission to help find a school for Julio. I ask the reference librarian for help and go sit at a library table with the sources that the librarian has located for me.

After hours of reading, I locate two schools that I think will be a good fit for Julio. Darlington School in Rome, Georgia, is a boarding school on more than 400 acres that contain woodland areas and lakes. The emphasis at Darlington is on character and service, and a full one hundred percent of their students go on to college. The other school, Marion Military Institute, wows me when I read their motto: "Truth, Honor, and Service." *Truth and Honor!* My thoughts return to Jonas Stockman and the place I first adopted this for my life's motto.

MMI is our country's oldest military junior college, and they offer the high school studies that Julio needs. The history of the school is fascinating. William Howard Taft served as president of the board of trustees during the time that he was also President of the United States. MMI was one of the first schools in the South to have a student government association and an honor system. The best thing about this school? It's in Alabama and only two hours away from Marshall.

Before I leave the library, I ask the reference librarian for help in locating information on Father Bryan O. Walsh. She leaves to locate sources and, after about five minutes, returns with two biographies and a few local magazines. I read that Father Walsh was born in 1930 in Portarlington, Ireland. He was ordained as a priest in St. Augustine, Florida, in 1954 and came to Miami in

1957. Father Walsh is the Spanish-speaking director of Catholic Welfare Services in Miami. Humph. Not a lot to go on.

I call Dad about the two schools. He tells me David has picked up the visa for Julio from the United States Embassy. That's part of the battle won.

David is getting involved with the whole movement to get children out of Cuba and to Miami. He is helping by quietly moving through the community and telling parents about his contact with James Baker. David has to be so careful. Anyone could report him to Castro, and I can't imagine what would happen to him if Castro knew what he was doing.

Monday turns out to be a glorious day. No Calculus. Our professor doesn't show. This is the way it works—if you go to class and wait for ten minutes and the professor doesn't show, you can leave class without being marked absent even though he may show up later. No student is gonna hang around. We all leave.

Since I'm free for an hour, I go to the J-school. Luke the Legend is sitting behind the anchors' desk working on a script. "Hey, Cotton! Come on over here. I've got time. Let me show you some talent skills."

As much as I despise him, I'd be crazy to turn him down. I say, "You mean the Legend has time to work with this little ole Alabama girl?"

"It's your lucky day, Cotton. Here, put on the lavaliere mike. Let's make this real. No, no, Cotton! It goes about four inches below your chin." Already he is getting under my skin.

"Willie is back in the control room. Hey Willie," Luke shouts.

Willie sticks his head out of the control room. "What do ya need, Luke?"

"Could you run the audio board for us? Ellen needs to do a sound check." Luke turns back to me to explain that Willie is going to listen as I read from a script and set my audio levels.

"Sure thing, Luke," answers Willie, ducking back into the control room. Ellen read the script if as she was on air until Willie yelled, "Got you."

"OK, good. Now, let's talk about your body language. You need to put your elbows on the desk and slightly lean toward the camera. The audience will think that what you are saying is important. There's a little urgency there."

I put my elbows on the curved anchor's desk. "Like this?"

"Yes, but you've got to square your body with the camera. You're looking into the camera, but your shoulders are turned sideways."

"OK, I get it."

"Let's talk about your eyes which, by the way, are a gorgeous shade of blue, Cotton."

"Yeah, right. What about the anchor's eyes?" I pretend not to notice the compliment.

"The anchor's eyes should always look directly into the camera when the anchor is on air. You're talking to your audience, and you have to maintain eye contact. No rolling eyes. An anchor rolling his eyes off to one side or the other during delivery is a big no-no. Every little gesture is magnified on television, so no rolling eyes, Ellen."

"Got it. What about eye contact when I'm on camera with you, but I'm not talking and you are?"

"That's called a two-shot, Ellen. When I'm on camera alone, it's a one-shot. Now, if you are lucky enough to be in a two-shot with me and I'm on air, you can do three things. You really need to do all three things during my delivery." I don't know any of this, of course, and I'm caught up in every word. I feel my heart skip a beat.

"You can look directly into the camera lens. You can look at me. You can look down at your script. Do one or do all three. Nothing's worse that a frozen anchor with a big smile who sits that way during the other anchor's entire story. Seriously, about the two-shot: a good director will open and close the show with a two-shot and use one-shots during the rest of the show."

"Anything else?" Ellen asks.

"Yeah. Let's talk about energy. Energy doesn't always translate on television. You have to overcompensate. The best way to show energy is to smile; show your teeth. There's a major difference between an opening shot when the anchor welcomes the viewer with a smile and an opening when the anchor is sullen. But, Ellen, no smiling when talking about funerals and famines. Do ya get it?"

"I got it, Luke. Thanks so much. Don't know that I want to be in front of the camera, but I need to know all this."

"Lose that Alabama accent, Cotton, and you'd probably do all right."

I leave the studio thinking he is the most egotistical person I know—certainly the best-looking one. I hurry to meet my roommate, Ann. She has agreed to go to see Father Walsh with me. We take the city bus to the Catholic Welfare Bureau at 395 First Street.

Ann says, "How do you even know he's gonna be there?

Why didn't you call him first?"

"I don't know, Ann. If this whole operation is a secret and I'm not even supposed to know about it, how can I just call him? I don't want to do anything to hurt Julio."

We ride the rest of the way in silence. *Think, Ellen. How much about Julio is necessary information?* The tall skyscrapers, and people walking on the sidewalk in a hurry, flash by as I plan for my visit with Father Walsh. It does register with me that a few men on the sidewalk are Cuban—men in linen Guayaberas and black trousers—evidence that men and women of Cuba are coming to Miami to escape Castro.

I see 395 First Street on the street sign outside and pull the dangling cord above my head. The bus stops and the door whooshes open. Ann and I step off the bus and stand on the sidewalk looking at the yellow stucco building labeled *Catholic Welfare Bureau.*

"Come on, Ann. Let's go."

We open the door to a pleasant room. Painted in pale yellow, the walls are covered with stunning black and white photos of children. I address a young secretary seated against the far wall. "Is Father Walsh in?"

"Your lucky day," she answers back. "He just came in. I'll see if he can see you. Your name?"

"Ellen Jones." I look at Ann and grimace. *What am I doing here? What do I think he'll tell me?*

I look up as a priest well over six feet walks into the room, looks at me, and smiles."Ellen Jones? Hello. Please, come into my office." He gestures toward the corner office. Ann and I follow him.

Father Walsh settles himself in his leather desk chair and indicates with his hand that I'm to sit across the worn cherry desk from him. "Now, how may I help you?" he asks.

I have decided how much I want to reveal and begin with the basics. "Father, my aunt is married to a Cuban with two children, Carlota and Julio. They are currently in Havana. We want Julio to visit us in Alabama during Christmas, so we're arranging for a travel visa."

"That sounds nice, but why come to me?"

"I'm worried about him getting here. He's coming on the twentieth of December. Perhaps you'll pray for him, Father?"

"What a coincidence! I'm picking up two children at the airport on that day—a boy and a girl. They're flying in from Cuba." He pauses and looks at me for a moment, then leans in toward me. "Ellen, let me tell you a story," he says.

"Last month a Cuban child flew into Miami. His parents sent him, thinking that relatives here in Miami would care for him. Little did they know that their American relatives were destitute and had no means to support the boy. He was passed from family to family. Finally, the boy, Pedro, reached our doors. He was a psychological wreck. He was skin and bones. We're caring for him and finding him a home. No child coming from Cuba will be hungry and alone if we can help it."

"Oh, Father. What an awful story. That won't happen to Julio. I'll meet him and take him straight to Alabama for Christmas. I'd just like it if you'll pray for him. He's got to get out of Cuba!"

"Ellen, I pray for all God's children. I'll pray especially for your Julio. God bless, my child."

"God bless you, too. Thank you Father."

Ann and I leave the building and hurry to catch the nasty-smelling bus as it idles at the curb. Ann has not said a word since we entered the welfare building forty minutes ago. She just listens as I repeatedly ask, "Did I do the right thing?"

Finally Ann says, "Give it a rest, Ellen." She punches me on my shoulder to show that she's not really upset.

I hug her. "Ann, thanks so much for going with me. I'd never have had the guts to go by myself."

November draws to a close, and I pack my bags to fly into Mobile two days before Thanksgiving. Dad picks me up at the airport, and we head straight for Callander. I love driving through Marshall on the way to the plantation. The streets are busy today.

I see Lewis Henry, editor and publisher of *The Marshall Times-Standard,* striding toward his shop. I wave out the window to get his attention. He has taught me so much about photography and research. I look forward to pulling up a stool at his old workbench and catching up on the *doings* in Marshall. If I don't make it to see him this visit, I'll go during Christmas for sure.

As Dad parks the car in front of our house, Aunt Essie comes flying out the door with her apron flapping. She says, "Ellen girl, I'm so excited to have you home for a few days!" I grab her and give her a big hug before she can break into the story of the Prodigal Son. Then I walk with her into the kitchen and beg her for a cup of her apple cider.

Sitting around the kitchen table, Essie and I try to talk at once, but Dad interrupts to say, "Hey, Ellen has the floor."

I tell them about my classes and time spent at the J-school. I try to explain the Twist to Essie. It's hopeless. I tell them about Ann and me going to see Father Walsh. "Dad, I don't know if it was the right thing to do," I say. "I just felt strongly that I needed to talk to him before Julio gets on that plane."

"Don't worry, Ellen," Dad says. "It can't hurt to have made contact with Father Walsh. You did the right thing."

Dad catches us up on what he knows about the Cuba situation. David has been trying for weeks to get an airline ticket for Julio. It's not so easy. Castro decided that no airline tickets out of Cuba would be purchased with Cuban pesos, so the route followed to get a ticket is circuitous indeed. Members of the American Chamber of Commerce in Havana help with the process, Dad explains. These are the very businessmen who had their businesses taken away from them by Castro. Now, the members make donations to the Catholic Welfare Bureau for the sole purpose of flying children out of Cuba. The Catholic Welfare Bureau then writes a check to American citizens living in Cuba. These American citizens purchase airfare tickets for the children by writing personal checks through the W. Henry Smith Travel Agency in Havana.

Cuba

children

Dad mentions that working through Mr. Baker, David finally manages to secure a ticket for Julio to fly out of Havana. God willing, Julio will be with us at Callander for Christmas.

Talk moves away from the Cuban situation. Essie tells me about the Marshall Garden Club's latest project, and she fills me in on Aunt Eleanor. Most of her conversation though is about her church circle going to Miss Mamie's after Sunday night service to watch her new color television. They never miss *The Ed Sullivan Show.* "That Elvis Presley can really sing, but none of us understands The Beatles," she reports. "Who lives in a yellow submarine?"

Amanda comes by the house while we're still sitting around the table. She seems genuinely glad to see me. Talk turns to the Thanksgiving meal—my favorite meal of the year by far. Amanda says, "I'm excited about bringing my oyster dressing.

Just wait! You'll just love it."

Silence.

Tradition ~~change~~.

Finally, Aunt Essie clears her throat and says, "Amanda, there must be some misunderstanding. In this house, we have cornbread dressing for Thanksgiving. It's my grandmother's recipe."

Amanda doesn't miss a beat. "If you've always had that dressing, Essie, it's time for a change. I'd love to bring my oyster dressing."

Uh oh! I look at Dad. He looks back at me. I shrug.

Dad says, "Amanda, I'm sure that your oyster dressing is wonderful. Why don't we have your dressing on Christmas Eve? It wouldn't be Thanksgiving without Essie's dressing."

Change

I've got to give Amanda credit. She says, "Oh, sure Will. I'll bring my cranberry relish with brandy in it for Thanksgiving then." Dad tells her that sounds perfect. Essie preens.

It's great to be back home. I've missed my room. I open the door and take it all in—the furniture with its coat of Forest of Ferns paint, the very white bedspread and curtains, and the bookcases topped with framed photos.

I walk over to a bookcase and pick up a photo—Jo Jo and me at prom. Look at that dress with its soft off-the-shoulder top and its skirt with layers of chiffon. I remember the day we all went to Mobile to buy it. Jo Jo and me—so happy and so young. It's been two years, but I feel so much older.

I smile when I spot the picture of Dad, Essie and me at my high school graduation. Dad is in his Sunday clothes, and Essie is wearing her best dress. They are brimming with pride. I place the photo back on the bookcase and get ready for bed. Aaah—so good to slide between the covers of my own bed.

I wake up when I hear the stairs creaking. I look at the clock; it's almost midnight. Aunt Essie is heading for the kitchen to put the turkey in the oven. The turkey will cook all night and will be done around ten in the morning. I scrunch down under my covers, loving that I'm at home, and Essie is in charge.

Waking up on Thanksgiving morning, I sniff the air. The smell that floats on the air holds the promise that a feast is coming. I can't get dressed fast enough.

I walk into the dining room. Would you look at the dining room table? It's covered with one of Grandmother Virginia's pure white quilts, and the plates on the table for Dad, Aunt Essie, Amanda, and me are the Franciscan wheat pattern, painted the color of caramel and featuring an identical shock of wheat in the center of each plate and bowl.

As a centerpiece, Essie has placed her corn-shuck dolls resembling Pilgrims with small orange and green pumpkins for added color. My throat tightens when I think of all the work Essie has put into this meal. Silently, I tell God I am thankful for Aunt Essie.

When Amanda, Essie, and I have loaded the table with turkey, dressing, gravy, sweet potato casserole, and pies of every variety, we call Dad to come to the table. We hold hands around the table, and Dad says the blessing. I love holding hands with my family each year, thanking God for all he has provided.

After the Thanksgiving meal, Amanda compliments Essie on the table and dressing then Essie compliments Amanda on her relish. I excuse myself to go pay my respects to Jonas Stockman. I never come to Callander without visiting Jonas.

No one knows the history of Jonas Stockman. Why is he buried on Callander land? I think about the inscription on his tombstone as I walk through the silence of late fall in the woods

Revolutionary War Soldier
Jonas Stockman
Born 1753, Died 1829
Truth and Honor

His grave stands all alone in a small clearing with hardwoods and pines and brambles all around it. Its marble surface is mottled. Looking closely, I see gray, dusty white, and green from mold. Surprisingly, it's standing straight up. Most old stones are leaning in one direction or another.

Reaching the grave, I brush the leaves off the grave mound and settle on the ground near the headstone. I lean over and trace the words *Truth and Honor* with my finger. The stone is so cold; my finger is numb before I finish moving through the swirls of the word, *Honor*. This is the biggest puzzle of all. Why *Truth and Honor?*

Aunt Zia and I used to stand at his grave and create stories about his life, imagining who he married and the children they bore. Since Zia has been in Cuba, I have visited the grave alone to talk to Jonas about my life and, most often, about my problems. I place a rock on the grave and promise Jonas I'll be back at Christmas.

Before I leave to go back to school, I sit on the edge of the bed in my bedroom. I open my much-read baby book and take out the paper with Luella's three predictions for my life.

She will be an advocate for the beauty.

She will foil a dictator.

She will find the soldier.

All my life I've read these predictions and considered them rubbish. Right up to my senior year in high school, anyway. That year, when I stood up for Neta Levy, who was not entered into the Miss Marshall Beauty Pageant because she was Jewish, everything changed. I think about how I surprised myself, denouncing the school board in my valedictorian speech at graduation. I stood up for Neta Levy in front of the entire crowd and in front of everyone in Marshall.

I defended Neta Levy, the beauty. Now, I give a little more credence to Luella's predictions. But find the soldier? Foil a dictator? Seems a little far-fetched to me.

Allusions

Chapter Thirteen: December 1960

L ast night, I went to my first concert. Ann and I saw The Kingston Trio perform. I'll never forget it. We were three rows back from front center. I tilted my head back and watched as they sang "It takes a worried man to sing a worried song. . ." The entire audience joined in as they sang, "Hang down your head Tom Dooley, hang down your head and cry—" It just doesn't get any better.

Today I got another letter from Aunt Essie. *Trouble, trouble, boil, and bubble!* Aunt Essie's furious with Amanda again. It seems this time Amanda is gonna disrupt Christmas. She and Daddy are leaving right after we open gifts and heading for Birmingham to visit Amanda's mother.

Aunt Essie thinks Dad is mesmerized with Amanda and can't think for himself. She closes the letter with a quote, and this one's not from the Bible, "The heat of the tail overpowers a man and turns his brain to mush. Essie Jones." I laugh out loud.

Well, Christmas should be interesting. I agree with Essie. This woman is disrupting our life and taking my daddy away. I mean, Christmas is sacred. You don't mess with Christmas!

But before getting to Christmas, we have to deal with Julio. Julio flies in tomorrow on a flight scheduled to leave Havana's José Martí Airport at 9:00 a.m., landing in Miami in less than an hour. I'm getting a rental car so I can pick Julio up, and we'll start the drive to Callander.

I take a taxi to the car rental station and, wouldn't you just know it, they don't have any record of my reservation. I'm chewing the inside of my mouth and walking the floor until, finally, they find a Chevrolet Bel Air available for rental. *Damn it! I'm gonna be late picking up Julio. He's gonna feel deserted.*

I get to the airport, park, and rush inside. No Julio. I search everywhere. I can't help thinking I've let everyone down—Dad, Aunt Zia, David, and, most of all, Julio.

On a hunch, I borrow a phone and call the Catholic Welfare Bureau. The young secretary we spoke with last month answers the phone. I'm shaking so badly I can hardly talk."Is Father Walsh there? This is Ellen Jones."

"No, Ellen. He picked up three children at Wilcox Field and drove to Kendall."

At first, my heart sinks. Then, I remember distinctly Father Walsh mentioning he would pick up *two* children, a boy and a girl. "Three children? Wasn't he supposed to pick up two children?"

The secretary replies, "You know, I think you're right—two children."

"But you said three. Maybe he has my nephew, Julio. How do I get to Kendall?"

She gives me directions and it takes about thirty minutes for me to get to Kendall from the airport. I see signs for Kendall and turn into the area. It's sandy and scruffy-looking with tall grass everywhere. A few lone, scraggly palm trees make a stand at the entrance. There are two large stucco buildings and a smaller one.

I pull up in front of one of the large buildings and immediately see Father Walsh with three children. My heart nearly leaps out of my chest when I realize one is Julio. I hear *ka-thump, ka-thump* as I just sit there staring at Julio. My mouth is dry. . .I can't move. Finally, Father Walsh notices and nudges Julio. Julio runs toward me.

"Ellen, Ellen. It's you!"

I get out of the car. I try to smile. My voice breaks.

"I've got you now, Julio."

He is trying not to cry. His lower lip trembles just a little. "Ellen, you know that I wasn't afraid."

"No, Julio. You're very brave. I would have been terrified." We smile at each other.

I turn to Father Walsh, square myself, and stand straight in front of him, like I'm doing penance. "Father, I'm so sorry." I'm trying hard not to cry. "I rented a car from this company weeks ago, and I got to the place early, Father. I really did."

"Ellen, don't worry yourself so. I knew there was a good reason you weren't there."

"But when I asked for a reservation for Ellen Jones, they denied having one. I was terrified Julio would think I had forgotten him."

Father says, "I am waiting at the airport, and I see all three children come off the plane together. The boy and girl here, Guillermo and Clara, have signs around their necks with their names written on them. No name on Julio."

"But how did you know, Father? How did you know the extra boy was Julio?"

"Why Clara told me, of course. We waited almost an hour before leaving the airport. I knew that something was wrong, so I just brought Julio along with me. Here, come meet Julio's new friends." Father Walsh introduces me to Guillermo and Clara. Both are younger than Julio.

"They'll be staying at Kendall because they have no relatives

Cuban Children refugees

in the United States. But they will be safe until their parents come," Father Walsh says.

The little girl pulls her hair back and says, "Look. My earrings. They couldn't see them for my hair." She has diamond studs in each ear, rather large diamond studs. Father Walsh explains that the soldiers take anything of value from the children before they get on the plane. Rather gutsy of this little girl to fool Castro's soldiers.

Father Walsh offers, "Come on, Ellen. I'll show you around."

I finally really look at my surroundings. It's obvious that the two-story white stucco building has some age on it. The building has four square columns in the middle and a cupola on top. It stretches off to the left and right, and on both sides each floor has about seven windows.

"This is the boy's dorm," Father Walsh says. "It was built in 1935 and, before we took over Kendall, it was a home for delinquent children. We are happy to have it for the Pedro Pan children."

Inside a large open space are rows of wooden cots made up with tightly tucked sheets. A red woolen blanket is folded at the end of each cot. It's a far cry from the mansions that line the streets in Miramar, but it's clean and it's safe. There's food, love, and safety here for these children.

Outside, I grab Father Walsh's hand. "How can I ever thank you, Father? God Bless you."

"Safe travels, Ellen," Father replies as he turns to the two children who traveled with Julio. I feel blessed to have met Father Walsh, and I thank God he was there to pick up Julio.

On our long drive to Callander, Julio tells the story of his travel adventure. "Ellen, Dad and Zia took me to the airport. We got there around eight o'clock. I had to leave Dad and Zia and go into a room all by myself. The top half of one wall was glass. Dad and Zia were watching me through the glass. We just waited. I could see this large clock on the wall, and the hands just barely moved, inching toward 9:00 a.m."

"I had my suitcase with me," he says. "It just had clothes in it. Dad told me the inspectors would take anything of value, so I could just take clothes with me."

Ellen says, "So you left Cuba with nothing important to you? Just clothes?"

Julio smiles and says, "Well, I had a picture of Dad, a picture of Carlota, and a picture of my grandparents stored away in my underwear." He smiles. "They didn't search me."

I smile back. What a brave thing to do.

"Julio, the other two children that I met were in the same room?"

"Yes. We didn't look at each other. We just sat and watched the clock. At nine o'clock a man in uniform told us we were ready to board the plane."

Ellen asks, "David and Zia were still outside the room?"

"Yes. I walked up to the window and put both my hands on the glass. Then Zia put her hand on my left, and my Dad put his hand on my right. They couldn't hear me so I mouthed to them that I loved them."

He's quiet for a minute. I can tell he's processing the day. "Getting on the plane was the hardest thing I've ever done," he says. "I had to concentrate on my feet—just walking to the plane. I didn't dare look back."

"Oh, Julio."

We ride for miles and miles without talking. I think of the horror of leaving the people you love, the country you love, your home—all you've really ever known. What a brave young man.

When we stop to spend the night, I find a phone and call Dad. I assure him that I have Julio, and we'll be at Callander tomorrow afternoon. I ask Dad to call David and Zia. They have to know that Julio is safe.

The next afternoon we drive onto Callander Plantation. Julio loved the plantation when he visited at Christmas two years ago, and he's excited to be back. He waves to some of the sharecroppers he remembers. We pull up in front of the house and before Julio is out the door, Dad grabs him in a tight hug. Finally, he passes Julio to Essie who is crying. There's no doubt as to Julio's welcome here.

As Julio blends into life at the plantation; I do the same. I walk the fields and visit Jonas Stockman. On schedule, I go to Marshall on Saturday. My first stop is at *The Marshall Times-Standard* building. I can't wait to see Lewis Henry.

I walk in the door and, as always, he invites me to join him at his long workbench. I climb up on a stool and say, "Oh Mr. Henry, I've really missed you."

"You know things are really dull without you, Ellen. I've missed you, too."

"Well, I'm here, and I'm ready for you to tell me all about Marshall. What's been happening?"

"The first and most important thing is that we've got a new school board. The old board's term was up this past September and not a single one of the old members were re-elected. I think you know why, young lady."

"Neta Levy?"

"Of course, Ellen. We're a small town in the backwater, but I'm proud to say that our citizens wouldn't stand for what old Mr. Wilson pulled. He and his wife have moved out of Marshall and gone to Georgia where they can live near her parents. Good riddance!"

My editorial about Neta Levy had been quite the scandal. I'm thrilled the school board is composed of new members.

I ask, "What about the Miss Marshall Pageant now?"

Change

"Word has it that it's totally restructured now. Girls are nominated, and the student body votes. Very simple."

"Oh, Mr. Henry. That's wonderful! Now, what about your photography? Got any great shots to show me?"

"Hold on. I've got a few that I took out West last summer."

Mr. Henry comes back with a handful of 8x10 photos. I shuffle through them one by one. They were taken at Jenny Lake near Jackson Hole, Wyoming. "Oh, Mr. Henry! You haven't lost your touch. These are magnificent!"

My favorite is a shot of the lake. The left half of the frame is filled with birch trees. It's a stunning shot.

Mr. Henry says, "Take that one, Ellen. I'd love for you to have it."

I get up, walk around the workbench, and kiss him on the cheek.

"Thank you so much. Well, gotta go meet Liz at the drugstore. So good to see you, Mr. Henry."

I enter the drugstore and stand for a minute to take it all in. On the left at the back of the store there's a scarred counter lined down the front with round, padded stools. When Liz and I were younger, we loved to sit on these same stools and whirl each other around.

Bobby Jenkins is standing behind the soda fountain, and I order a Cherry Coke. I always liked to watch the soda jerks pull down the shiny spigot to release the bubbly Coke.

Five cherry red leather booths are lined up on the right side of the room, and their tables are covered with names that have been carved into them. Liz is seated in one of the booths.

I pick up my Cherry Coke at the fountain counter and sit down across from Liz. She's grinning. "Gosh, you look great, Ellen! Miami agrees with ya."

"You haven't changed a bit, Liz. I'm dying to hear about you. How do you like your sophomore year at Marshall College?"

"You know, Ellen, I really love it. I want to teach high school English. Who knows? I may end up back at Marshall High."

"Wouldn't that be something?" I say. "You could take Miss Taylor's place. If she ever retires that is. Think of all those kids who would love you like I loved Miss Taylor. It's a special job, Liz."

"Well, it's something to think about. In the meantime, I'm having a great time at Marshall. There are a couple of guys that I'm dating. I can't decide between the two. Like I said, I'm having fun!"

"Good for you. Tell me what's happening around here."

"I hear that Jo Jo Reed is coming home for Christmas tomorrow. That excite you? It sure excites Mable Johnson."

"I forgot about Mable. Is she still obnoxious?"

"Does the sun shine? Of course she is."

"Ugh. Well, at least I don't have to see her." After telling Liz about Columbus and the J-school, I leave with a promise to see her again before I head back to school.

When I get back home, I rope Julio into going with me to search for this year's Christmas tree. We always get a cedar tree and decorate it with my mother's favorite ornaments—Shiny Brite birds with plastic brush tails.

Tradition

Julio and I tromp for what seems like miles before we spot the perfect tree. It has a straight trunk—a major requirement for a Jones tree. We saw it down, and Julio is gracious enough to carry it on his shoulder back to the house.

We set up the tree after supper and put Mother's birds on the tree. We also put multi-colored bubble lights and tinsel. My inclination is to stand back and throw bunches of tinsel at the tree, but, in honor of my mother, I put the tinsel on one strand at a time.

Tradition / Honor

We all go into Marshall on Christmas Eve for the 6:00 p.m. service. There's a live nativity in front of the church. I remember just three years ago Mother was Mary and Dad was Joseph. We walk into the church, and each of us is given a candle.

The service is wonderful. I never tire of hearing the Christmas story. My favorite part of the service is at the end. We light our candles and hold them high as we sing *Silent Night, Holy Night*. Tears roll down my face as I think of my mother. She should be here. Dad reaches over and squeezes my hand.

Tradition

Christmas morning I wake up smelling coffee Essie is brewing. I walk into the kitchen where she is whipping eggs for our favorite breakfast: French toast. After breakfast we're sitting around the table talking when the doorbell rings.

I say, "I'll get it!"

I open the door to Amanda who is standing on the porch with her arms loaded with gifts. I resent the fact she's taking Dad away on Christmas day. Still, I know I have to be nice. I give her an air kiss and invite her in.

We gather around the tree and get comfortable. The melee begins as we all open gifts at once. The last gift I open is from Amanda. It's a small box, elegantly wrapped. I take my time peeling off the bow and removing the paper. I hold in my hand a jeweler's box. Inside is a beautiful opal ring.

Amanda says, "Opals are for Libras, Ellen. I'm a Libra, too. My parents gave me this ring when I turned sixteen. Now I want you to have it."

Well, just damn. Every time I'm prepared to hate her, she does something like this.

I stand up, walk across the room, and hug her. I don't imagine that it was easy for her to give the ring away. I am so touched— but not so touched that I don't resent it like crazy when she and Dad leave for Birmingham. I try. I smile and wish them safe travels and say inane things like, "Give your mother our regards." I don't even know her mother. I barely even know Amanda.

Essie says, "When my father and my mother forsake me, then the Lord will take me up. Psalm 27:10." Somehow, it is a comfort.

On Christmas night the family and all the sharecroppers, with their families in tow, attend the annual eggnog party that my grandfather, David Henry Callander, holds at the plantation house. I'm proud to have David Henry as my grandfather.

There are eleven sharecropper families at Callander, and what a mixed bunch. Seven of the eleven families are white and four are colored. Callander is a magical place indeed, and we live in a sort of bubble, isolated from the terrible racial sickness swirling through our country. I wouldn't trade it for the world.

Our sharecroppers rarely leave Callander except for church and, of course, the children go to school. The sharecroppers grow everything they need to eat, or they buy it at the Callander commissary. If they need a doctor, my grandfather has the doctor come to them. I used to think David Henry sheltered the people who work on Callander from the outside world. Now I see all of us have been blessed to live on Callander land. We're so lucky.

Sharecroppers

The Christmas party at the plantation house is the party of the year. All the sharecroppers, colored and white, come and bring their families. That means the Reed family will be there and that means Jo Jo Reed will be there.

Racial Toleration

I don't understand my feelings for Jo Jo. We grew up together, played together. Then, my senior year in high school things changed. I started getting these funny feelings about Jo Jo and loved it when he kissed me that night. He wrote a poem for me and actually gave it to me at the Christmas eggnog party two years ago. I still have that poem. Don't think I'll ever get rid of it.

Christmas night Aunt Essie, Julio, and I ride over to the plantation house. I get a lump in my throat when I see lit candles in all the windows of the house. The pure white candles stand out like signals of love and welcome.

Tradition

In the great hall at Callander, the eggnog is flowing. I give David Henry Callander a huge Christmas hug. I have to stand on tiptoe to hug him. He's very tall, like all the Callanders before him.

He asks, "Where's your father?" I tactfully explain that Dad and Amanda had to go to Birmingham. Essie snorts.

I look down the hall, past the eight-foot cedar tree filled with ornaments and colored lights. There stands Jo Jo Reed in his Air Force Academy uniform. I am mesmerized. He grins at me, and I turn to jelly.

Did God ever create a more gorgeous human being? I don't think so.

I walk up to Jo Jo to give him a quick hug, but he picks me up and twirls me around instead. "Ellen, you look amazing!"

In David Henry's library, we settle into the large overstuffed chairs that face the desk.

"Oh, Ellen, it's so good to be back on Callander land. I've missed it. How can you love two places so fiercely? I love Colorado, too, but this place is special."

"What's it like out there?" I ask.

"It has a feel to it that I can't quite describe. I feel I'm at home and all my ancestors would have been at home there. There's a feeling of time stretching backwards, like I have old ties to the land. Strange, huh?"

"Well, I assure you that I don't feel that way about Miami. I love the university and always will. Wish you could come meet my friend, Ann, and all the people in the broadcast journalism department. They treat me like one of them even though I really can't be in the department officially until next year."

"They sound nice. So, Ellen, would you like to see Colorado?"

"Sure, I'd love it. Never been anywhere but Alabama and Florida."

"Well, there's a cadet dance coming up in May. I'm required to go and wouldn't mind going if you were there to go with me."

"Let me check on the price of a ticket to fly out. I'll let you know."

"Gee, Ellen. I didn't think of that. I'm so embarrassed; I should be buying your ticket, but I'm sure you know that I can't afford it."

"Oh Jo Jo, don't fret so. Someday you will be a general, and I'll expect you to pay every time we get together."

"You bet. Well, think about the dance and let me know. I can make arrangements for you to stay on campus, and I promise to feed you. If you can swing the ticket, I'll take care of everything else."

"I'll talk to Dad, and I'll let you know in January, Jo Jo. Promise." We sit for a moment, just enjoying each other's company.

I am first to break the silence. "Well, we better get back inside. Aunt Essie is not a happy person. No telling how many people she's offended by now. I'd better go check on her."

Jo Jo stands up and reaches for my hand. He pulls me close and kisses me. I kiss him back.

Essie and I leave Julio to the eggnog. David Henry promises to deliver him home. And he does. When I get up the next morning, Julio is sitting at the kitchen table drinking coffee.

I ask, "Have a good time last night?"

"Yes, I did. I spent a lot of time talking to Jo Jo after you left. He told me some things that will get me ready for MMI. You know that I leave next week?"

"Yes, I know. I've never been to Marion but hear there are tons of beautiful old homes there. There's also another college that's strictly female. That interest you?"

"I'm just worried about learning the ropes. No time to think about *las señoritas*."

"Whatever you say, Julio. Our family loves you. You stay in touch with us, and we'll come anytime you need us."

"Thanks, Ellen. That means a lot. I promise to write."

Dad and Amanda return home that afternoon. The atmosphere in the house is a little chilly, so I decide to go back to Miami before New Year's Eve. Before I leave, Dad and I talk about the dance in May. Dad thinks that I should go. He even agrees to buy the ticket if it's not too much.

"Thank you, Dad. You know that you don't have to do that, but I'd love to visit Colorado. And see Jo Jo—that's part of it." I grin at Dad.

"You not getting serious about Jo Jo, are you?" Dad asks.

"Well, Dad. I like him a lot—always have, but serious? No, not serious."

Dad says, "Oh, and one other thing. Amanda and I talked on the way back from Birmingham. We'd like to fly down to Miami for Valentine's Day. That OK with you?"

"Do you have to ask? You know I'll love it. I'll tell all those boys on campus who are lined up to ask me out that I'm taken for Valentine's Day."

"Well, Sugar, we'll see you in February then."

Chapter Fourteen: January 1961

I'm excited about the new semester at Columbus. Except for Art 101. Unlike my mother, I have no talent for drawing or painting. On the first day of class the professor says, "Stand up. We're going for a walk."

I can see by everyone's facial expressions that they are thinking what I'm thinking: *What is this?* We walk outside the building to the round, stone water tower. It's a tall, gray cylinder standing on its end.

Professor Walker says, "Now students, please look at the tower and tell me what color it is. Raise your hand when you're ready."

I raise my hand. "Gray," I say.

The professor answers, "Yes, gray is one of the colors on the tower but look again."

One of the other students raises their hand and says, "Hey, I see orange."

I really look at the tower. I see orange dripping down from the top—maybe some kind of rust? I see various shades of green moss, and I see black. From mold, maybe? I am wowed. I've walked by that tower every day for two and a half years and only noticed gray.

"I'm sure you know why we spent our first day with this exercise," says Professor Walker. "You can't paint an object unless you really see it."

You know, I think I'm going to like art. I sure like the teacher.

What I don't like is the news from Cuba about Carlota. It seems she will be teaching as well. Castro's latest project is called the Cuban Literacy Campaign, designed to reduce the high illiteracy rate in Cuba. The majority of peasant families are illiterate, meaning that they cannot even read on a first-grade level.

Castro is identifying the illiterate citizens across Cuba and plans to form literacy brigades to go out and teach them. Educated Cubans, especially students from urban backgrounds, have been encouraged to join the literacy brigades. If you have a sixth-grade education or better, you can volunteer.

Aunt Zia writes that she is afraid Carlota will volunteer to go. Carlota's personality has not changed. She's still as argumentative as ever. She's been exposed to Castro's Marxist theories because they permeate the very air of Havana.

Who was Marx? He was an atheist who developed a political theory called communism, believing that most properties should be owned by the government and people should be paid based on their needs. Imagine not owning your own home or car. Imagine not worshipping in the church of your choice. Karl Marx did not think highly of the individual and his ability to excel.

It would be just like Carlota to volunteer to teach the peasants, I think. She has such a strong personality. It's not wrong that she's teaching citizens to read. That's commendable. I just hate to see her teaching communist doctrine.

Speaking of strong personalities, I got a letter from Amanda today, too. It's a letter of apology. Again. She writes that she's sorry that our Christmas afternoon was disrupted. She says she knows how important a family Christmas is. For the first time, I learn her mother is in a Birmingham nursing home in Birmingham. Amanda's father is no longer living, and Amanda is an only child. She did not want her mother to be alone on

Christmas Day.

Well, damn! Who in their right mind could criticize Amanda for wanting to be with her mother on Christmas Day? Why did she have to be so private? Why didn't she just explain instead of taking Dad away leaving Essie and me to stew? Did she ever think of bringing her mother to Callander? Think I'll stew a little more about this.

Change ~ Christmas

I forget the letter as I walk into the J-building, ready for duty. The news show is five minutes out. I grab camera one. It's so good to be back with the camera handles in my hand. For once, the show goes off smoothly. No stress. Until Luke walks up, that is.

"Hey, Maid of Cotton. I actually missed you over the holidays. I missed you so much that I'd like to take you to the movies tomorrow night. *North by Northwest* is playing. You might get so scared that you'll hold my hand."

"Why Luke, are you asking me on a date?"

"Yes, Cotton, I guess I am!"

I grin. "Then I'd love to go," I say.

I am a lucky girl, I think to myself as I head out of the studio later. I'm going on a date with Luke the Legend, and I'm going to a cadet dance with Jo Jo Reed. I need to buy a ticket to Colorado Springs and write to Jo Jo to let him know. Dad sent me money to buy the ticket.

I make a return trip to the Miami airport and purchase a ticket. Such a happy time compared to when I was there to pick up Julio. The ticket cost Dad as much as one whole semester of tuition at Columbus University. I feel guilty, really guilty, about the cost. Maybe when I'm working I can pay him back?

I write Jo Jo a long letter about life at Columbus, and I tell him that I have the ticket. I'll be flying into the airport at Denver on the fifth of May. I promise to bring a stunning dress with me. I want to look great at the dance. I'll take Jo Jo's breath away!

I love Art 101 more and more. We're learning about composition, and I can see how the rules used for composition in painting also apply to photography and film. Two rules that are most important to me are _Leading Looks_ and _Rule of Thirds_. The Rule of Thirds involves using imaginary lines to divide your canvas into thirds horizontally and vertically. What you have looks like tic-tac-toe.

You can use the lines to compose your landscapes or long shots so that your center(s) of interest falls on the lines themselves or where the lines intersect. Your shot will be more interesting than a shot where your center of interest is placed in the middle. We learn to use the grid to compose close-ups of subjects.

Notice in this shot of Jo Jo that the eyes of the subject are on the top line or, in other words, a third of the way down the grid. Eyes should not be in the center of the shot; the result would be too much headroom. This is the Rule of Thirds.

Composition rule number two involves lead room, which is also called nose room. When drawing or shooting a profile of a person, allow empty space in the direction the person is looking. This also applies to side views of cars driving down the road or football players running down the field and any shot that shows a side view of the subject. In the car example, more space is allowed in front of the car. The car needs room to move forward in the picture.

In television, lead room is important in interviews. The interviewee should look eyes right or eyes left, not directly into the camera lens. Lead room is provided so that the interviewee has room to look into the frame.

I think about Lewis Henry and his love of photography. I can't wait to talk about what I've learned with him. I want to look at his shots again now that I know more about composition. Think I'll borrow a camera from the J-school and go out and shoot.

Chapter Fifteen: February 1961

Castro — assassination attempt

I'm watching the news in the J-building and see that an attempt has been made on Castro's life. Eight gunmen were dropped off on the eastern shore of Cuba. Their intent was to ambush Castro as he was riding in a caravan to Santiago Cemetery, where Castro was set to speak at a graveside service.

Castro

According to the news story, it was pouring rain. The gunmen spotted the caravan and saw Castro's chief bodyguard riding in the front seat of the second car. The gunmen assumed Castro was in the rear seat and riddled the car with bullets, killing all in the vehicle. But it turns out Castro was riding in the next to last car and was not harmed at all. What a terrible time to live in Cuba.

I know Julio worries about his family. I decide to give him a call. He sounds happy and adjusted—if one can sound adjusted. He has stories to tell.

"Ellen, you won't believe this! Most of us cadets go to the movies on Sunday afternoon. It's more than the movies though. It's a dating service."

Dating Cadets

"Julio, whatever are you talking about?"

"There's an usher at the movies," he explains. "He's a young local man who walks down the two aisles of the theater looking for attractive girls. When he spots one, he leans over and quietly asks her if she minds a cadet sitting with her throughout the movie."

"You're kidding!"

"No. And if the girl says yes, which they usually do, the

usher chooses a cadet and walks him over to sit by the chosen girl. No kidding."

"Have you been involved in this?"

"Sure, Ellen. I watched *Breakfast at Tiffany's* with a girl from Judson College and *Splendor in the Grass* with the homecoming queen at the high school."

"My gosh, Julio! *Splendor in the Grass?*" I change the subject. "Maybe we'd better chat about Callander. How are things?"

I catch Julio up on the news I have from home and tell him about my trip to Colorado Springs in May. I tell him about Dad and Amanda. I wish him a Happy Valentine's Day. Don't think he has much of a problem in that department.

As promised, Dad and Amanda come for Valentine's Day. I pick them up at the airport, and we go by the Catholic Welfare Center. I have made an appointment with Father Walsh. Dad really wants to meet him.

It's good to see the Father again. While he and Dad talk, I tell Amanda about Aunt Zia. I tell her about her early career and about CBS sending her to Cuba to interview Batista. I tell her about Zia meeting and marrying David and remaining in Cuba. It's a great story. I'm sure Dad probably told her all this, but she pretends to be hearing it for the first time.

When we leave the Catholic Welfare Center, we drive to campus. I ask Dad and Amanda if Luke can come with us to eat. This time, we are going to the beach and we are having Tres Leches. I feel a little selfish, but hey, I've earned it!

We pick Luke up in front of the J-building and drive to South Beach. It's fun to just sit and talk. I really do feel blessed to have Dad, and even Amanda, here with me on Valentine's Day. Dad tells a funny story about the valentines I used to make for him. Amanda talks about her early interest in broadcast journalism. Luke is really interested in this and asks lots of questions. Who would have thought ole obnoxious Luke could fit in with Amanda and Dad so well?

I'm really enjoying this, but it's time to go. Dad and Amanda have to catch an evening flight. Luke goes with me to take them back to the airport. On the way back to campus, he tells me how much he likes Amanda. I wish he had known my mother.

I get a letter from Aunt Zia the next day. Carlota has done it. She's joined the Literacy Brigade. She was given books, one pair of boots, two pairs of socks, a beret, two pairs of pants, two shirts, and a blanket to sleep on. She was given a gas lantern, so that she could teach at night.

Cuba
Literacy
Brigade

She's living with a family somewhere in the countryside. Zia and David don't know where. The parents, grandparents, and three children all live in the house. Now Carlota lives there, too.

During the day Carlota works with the grandparents, teaching them to read. Many days, she goes into the fields to work with the parents and children. At night, she teaches the parents and children to read. The children learn quickly, while the parents are slower to learn, says Zia.

I notice there is no personal comment from Zia. Not one word of complaint against what Carlota is doing. I know Zia and David do not approve. This scares me. *What's happening?* I sure cannot see snooty, complaining Carlota working in the fields. The world is turned upside down in Cuba.

Upside down world

It's turned upside down on Columbus campus as well. Cynthia Farmer violated broadcast ethics by airing a story before checking her sources. Her lead was as follows:

Who: President of Columbus University, Dr. Paul Grady
What: Involved in a wreck and arrested for drunk driving, *When*:
Saturday, February 11, and *Where*: Coral Gables.

It seems President Grady had a mild stroke while driving and
ran into a car driven by a young mother with two children in the
car. The mother and her children were not hurt. President Grady
spent two nights in the hospital for tests and is now home.

Cynthia's story came from one witness, who not only saw
the wreck but also saw the police take President Grady away. She
had only one source, and an unreliable source at that! Dr. Shelby
is making a decision as to whether she will be removed from
the broadcasting program. She'll certainly never be an anchor on
Miami News Now again.

Dr. Shelby gathers the staff together and asks me to come as
well. I'll never forget his words. "First, it is our job to report the
news—to report the truth. Second, always use two sources and
do your best to verify their stories. Third, give the subject of the
news story a chance to respond to allegations of wrongdoing."

If Cynthia had spoken to the police, they would have refuted
the eyewitness account of what happened. If she had even tried
to talk to President Grady, she would have learned the truth. This
story was sensational, and, I'm sure, Cynthia thought she had the
story of her young life. She has probably ruined her chance of
being a broadcast journalist.

"Remember this and remember it well. Perform your job
ethically. Report the truth as far as you can ascertain that truth,"
Dr. Shelby adds.

Truth and Honor.

That night I'm restless. I sit in my dorm room and try to
study, but all I can think about is Dr. Shelby's speech. *Could that*

have been me? I'm shaken to my core. I hear the phone on the hall ring.

"Ellen Jones, phone," someone calls out. I pick up the receiver in the old, wooden booth. It's Luke.

"Cotton. I know you are up there brooding. Come to The Bowl with me." The Bowl is a green space on campus that is actually shaped like a bowl. It's where all the couples go to make out. I don't even have to think about it.

"I'll be right down," I say.

Luke has a red and blue blanket under his arm. I grab the other arm, and we quietly walk to The Bowl. Luke picks a spot where we seem to be alone, but I know there are other students in the Bowl; I can hear quiet murmurings and a girl laughing. I can see the burning tip of a cigarette off to our right, and I get a faint whiff of the cloying smell.

He spreads the blanket out for us to sit on. It's rough—maybe wool. Luke plops down on the blanket, and I sit close to him—close enough to smell the woodsy, leathery smell of his cologne. I glance at his profile—dark hair, square jaw, very handsome. I can tell you it's a powerful thing, being on a blanket in the Bowl with Luke O'Neal.

He wants to talk, so we talk about life turning on a dime and how scary it is to think about making a mistake like Cynthia made. We talk about where we're going now and where we want our lives to go.

Luke leans over. "Hey, Cotton. I think I'd like you to go with me wherever I go. I'm thinking that I love you."

Love? My gosh! That came from left field! What do I do? I lean in and kiss him, of course. I don't say anything. I just kiss him. For a long time.

The memory of the kiss lingers until the next day. I've got Luke's confession and Aunt Zia's letter on my mind. I know that normally Zia would be complaining about Carlota living with peasants in the countryside and teaching Marxist doctrine, but her letter is puzzling. I call and make an appointment with Father Walsh for the next day. Maybe he can help me sort it out and reassure me that Zia is OK.

The next day I'm back in his office. "Father," I say, "Aunt Zia would not have sent a letter like this without complaining about Carlota's involvement in the Literacy Brigade. It really worries me."

"Ellen, have you considered that David and your Aunt Zia are very worried about Carlota but are afraid to write about it? Telephone calls and personal mail are being monitored. She's wise to not say anything further. I'm sure that she thought you would get the message."

"That's terrible, Father Walsh. No freedom at all!"

"That's right, Ellen. Why do you think all those Cuban parents are sending their children to me? They don't want their children indoctrinated to become communists or, heaven forbid, be sent to the Soviet Union for their training and education."

"How is that going? Are children still flying over from Cuba?"

"Of course! Around 4,000 have arrived by last count. I don't know what the count is today."

"All those children. All those brave parents."

"Ellen, I have to caution you. Please don't talk about the organization outside your family. It's not publicized. We're trying to keep it secret and that is getting harder and harder. Castro closed the American Embassy last month, which creates a problem with getting student visas."

"What are you going to do, Father Walsh?"

"The State Department has given me blanket authority to issue visa waivers for children ages six to sixteen. In other words, they can travel here without a visa. This really helps because there are still so many children in Cuba that we need to bring over."

"We're calling this Operation Pedro Pan after that first child who came into our office. Please remember, Ellen, that what I've told you is confidential."

"I promise, Father. If it's alright, I'll tell Dad but no one else. Oh, Father, how lucky we were to get Julio out of Cuba!" I say.

Chapter Sixteen: March 1961

Father Walsh calls and asks if he can see me. How odd. I know something is wrong, I can hear it in his voice. I just can't imagine why he would come to campus to see me. I wonder what he has to say. I nervously brush my hair and put on lipstick before I go down to the lobby to wait for him.

He comes through the main dorm door and stops where I'm standing—my voice trembles. "Father Walsh?"

"Ellen, God bless you. Thank you for letting me come to see you."

"What's wrong, Father? Is it Carlota?"

"No, Ellen. It's your Aunt Zia. Mr. Baker helped David send this letter in the diplomatic pouch. I just got the letter this morning. You know David has to be careful what he writes."

"What is it, Father? What about Aunt Zia?"

"You'd better read David's letter, Ellen."

I shake my head. "No. I can't! You've got to tell me."

"Let's go sit down on one of those sofas. It's more private."

We move over to one of the quiet areas in the lobby, and I sink into the old sofa, waiting to hear about David's letter.

"Well child, David writes that Zia had become extremely afraid of the militia in Havana. Her first experience with them was when they taunted families coming out of the churches. Last month, Zia was riding home on the bus—she didn't do that often because the militias ride the buses. Well, two different militiamen spat on her as she stood up to walk off the bus."

"No. Aunt Zia is so proud. I can't imagine anyone spitting on her."

"David says in the letter that she rarely goes out now. On Monday, David was out of town, and Zia was alone. She looked out the window and saw the militiamen turning onto their street in marching formation. It scared her so badly that she ran out the front door. David's friend, Jorge, owns the restaurant across the street, and Zia ran over there."

"I understand why she would be afraid. She was alone," I say.

"Well, unfortunately, she would have been fine if she had not run. The militia was on a normal patrol through Miramar, not looking for anything in particular. Zia's running to the restaurant looked suspicious."

"I see that Father, but what's wrong? What happened?"

"Zia didn't notice the sign on the restaurant door: *Closed*. She didn't want to be alone. That's all she could think about. She barreled right into the restaurant, looking for Jorge. What she did not know, could not have known, was that a group of Cuban revolutionaries and our men from the CIA were plotting the assassination of Castro in a back room of the restaurant—"

"—So what happened, Father Walsh? Is Zia alive?"

"Yes. Zia is alive, but she is in La Cabaña prison. I don't really know which is worse—death or La Cabaña. But I'm getting ahead of myself. When the militiamen discovered the plotters, they opened fire. The leader of the plot was wounded and two of the men sent by the CIA were killed. The survivors have been taken to La Cabaña along with your Aunt Zia."

"What will happen, Father? Do they think Zia is guilty? That she is involved in this plot? They won't execute her, will they, Father?"

"*¿Quién sabe?* Who knows? Hopefully, David's status with Castro will save her. It's in David's hands now. He's got to get her out of La Cabaña."

"Father, I'd like to talk to David. Is it possible to reach him?" I ask.

"You'd have to schedule a call to David, but I think that can be arranged. His address and telephone number are right here on the letter. Come to my office on Saturday. I'll try to get a call through to David."

Everything is a blur for the rest of the week. I'm going through the motions: going to class, going to the J-building, going out to eat. I'm just living for Saturday. Every day, all day, I am wringing my hands and waiting for Saturday to come.

I go to the movies with Luke. We see *North to Alaska* with John Wayne—his choice, not mine. Luke knows something is wrong. He holds my hand throughout the movie. He doesn't ask what's wrong, but he tucks me under his arm on the walk back to the dorm. He has not mentioned that he loves me since our trip to The Bowl. I haven't mentioned it either.

Luke does mention spring break. "Hey, Ellen," he says, "Some of us broadcast people are going to Jamaica for spring break. Why don't ya come go with us? It would be too cool!"

"Gosh, Luke! How am I supposed to afford that? Are you gonna buy my ticket and pay for my hotel room?"

Aw, Ellen, you know that I would if I could. I can barely afford to go myself, but hey, it's my junior year. I think I deserve this trip!"

"Of course! You're Luke the Legend." I smile, but my mind is still on Saturday.

Finally, Saturday is here. I take the bus to the Catholic Welfare Bureau, and Father Walsh is there waiting for me. He picks up the telephone and dials the operator. The operator connects us to the long distance office then another operator in the long distance office connects us to the long distance office in Havana. Finally, the Havana operator promises to connect us to David's phone and call us back when the connection is made.

We wait. Then, the phone rings, and David is on the other line.

My words tumble all over each other, "Oh, David. How is Zia? Is she still in La Cabaña? This is terrible!"

"Ellen, wait. Zia's with me. Castro actually intervened with Che Guevara, who is in charge of La Cabaña. I was able to go to La Cabaña and get Zia though I didn't get her before she saw conspirators executed by a firing squad. They made her watch, Ellen. It was at night. Prisoners were led out and lined up against a wall lit with bright floodlights. Zia could see bullet holes in the wall from previous executions. She could hear music from a street carnival floating over the wall as the bullets ripped into the bodies of the conspirators. She's in really bad shape, Ellen. I have to get her out."

"What do you mean 'bad shape'?"

"She's not responding to me. She hasn't said a word since I brought her home from La Cabaña. She hums a song and doesn't talk. I'm really scared, Ellen."

"David, what can I do? How can we stay in touch?"

"It's easier for me to call you. I'll call next Saturday. Should I call you at this number?"

I ask, "Father, is this OK with you? Can David call here?"

Father Walsh responds, "Of course, Ellen. Saturday is the best time for him to call. No office staff is here on Saturdays. We'll be alone."

"David? This number is fine. What time?"

"Let's do noon. In the meantime, please pray for us. I'll talk to you next week."

I hang up the phone slowly and turn to Father Walsh, "Father, Zia is home with David, but she saw some things in La Cabaña that no one should see. After babbling about the executions when David first picked her up, she's stopped communicating. I'm so worried, Father."

"Well, child, thank God David was able to get her out of La Cabaña. That's a dark, evil place."

"She really needs to be at Callander."

"Ellen, it doesn't sound like she can travel alone. David would have to bring her home or someone would have to go get her, and that's no solution."

"There's got to be a way, Father. I'll think, and I'll see you next Saturday. Thank you for all you have done for our family. It is such a comfort."

I'm in the J-building on Monday for the newscast. The lead story is about a United States citizen who has been sentenced to prison for traveling to Cuba without a license. The U.S. frowns on its citizens traveling to Cuba, to the point that violators can be imprisoned and fined up to $250,000 each. The citizen is this case was trying to reconnect with his girlfriend.

Ban on travel to Cuba

I listen intently. I realize that I've been subconsciously rolling the idea of rescuing Zia around in my head. *How do I think that I can do that?* I have no idea.

That night Dad calls. Strange thing. Amanda wants to fly down to talk with me on Tuesday. She wants to take me to lunch. . .that's weird. *What could possibly be so important that Amanda would get on a plane to come see me alone?*

Chapter Seventeen: April 1961

I meet Amanda at the airport, and we drive to Coral Gables for lunch. We are back at the restaurant where we celebrated my birthday. Fine with me this time.

"Ellen, I know that you wonder why I'm here. I'm gonna shoot straight with you. Your dad and I want to get married, and I feel I need to ask for your blessing."

It's not like I haven't thought of this. It hurts, though. It's one thing to see Amanda with my father when it used to be my mother, but it's another thing altogether to see them married. . .there's more.

"Ellen, we want to get married at Callander plantation house in May," she says, "but, we are not going to do that unless we have your approval. We'd like Essie's approval too, and she will no doubt be influenced by your reaction. I won't do anything to coerce you. I don't want you to feel any pressure. I love your father, and he loves me. We can be happy together. Just like any couple, we will have bumps to cross over, but we are both ready to take this journey."

I don't respond to Amanda. *Truth and Honor.* I've got to think this through, but I have to be honest with myself and Amanda. I tell her I will think about how I feel. We talk about other things, like Luke and the broadcasting department.

I drive Amanda back to the airport and, on the way, I make a decision and I know it's the right decision. As Amanda gets out of the car to walk into the airport, I stand up on the driver's side of the car. Looking across the top I say, "Amanda, just one thing. I get to be the maid of honor."

She puts her hands up to her face and cries. I walk around the car and grab her into a tight hug. "It's OK, Amanda. Don't cry. This is a happy thing. I'm happy for you and Dad."

I drive back to campus. I feel really good knowing for sure I did the right thing. *Uh oh!* Now I've got to work on Essie. I wonder if she'll move back to town. I sure can't see her sharing the Callander house with Amanda.

That night I make a call to Callander. "Dad, I want you to know that I'm happy for you. Amanda says I can be maid of honor."

"Sure, Ellen. I wouldn't have it any other way. I sure do miss you. I may not be able to wait 'til May to see you again."

It's funny. In talking back and forth with Dad, I never once mention Zia. Something's telling me to keep it to myself. I hope that I'm doing the right thing with that, too.

I go to the welfare bureau building about fifteen minutes early on Saturday. Father Walsh and I talk about general things until the telephone rings at noon. It's David.

"Ellen. So good to hear your voice!"

"Hi, David. How are things? How is Aunt Zia?"

"Pretty much the same as last week. She's still not communicating with me. I'm at my wit's end."

"You know, David, I've done nothing but think about you and Zia. If I could blink my eyes and have her appear at Callander, I would. I think it would be good for her."

David says, "That goes without saying. I know that she needs to get out of Cuba. I don't want to let her go, but I will. She's pitiful right now."

I know I am taking a chance with what I say next. Our call may be monitored, but I'm desperate to help Aunt Zia. "David, if you can work it out, I'll come into Cuba and get her." *What the hell am I saying?*

Rescue Zia

David says, "I'll be in touch with you, Ellen. Have you talked to your Dad?"

"Yes, actually. I congratulated him on his upcoming wedding in May. If you're asking if I told him about Zia, no, I did not. I haven't contacted Julio, either."

"Let's leave it that way. I'll be in touch."

The last thing that I want to do is to talk to Essie, but it's gotta be done. Back at campus, I call home and Essie answers the telephone.

"Essie, it's me, Ellen."

"Oh, child, how wonderful to hear your voice today. I'm in a nervous state!"

"What's wrong, Essie?"

"Your father and Amanda are getting married next month and that leaves me no time to get the plantation house ready for the wedding."

Dead silence. I have no idea what to say.

"Can you believe that Amanda wants me to decorate Callander house? I've never felt so honored!"

Honor - Aunt Essie

I smile in amazement. "Essie, you always work miracles. You can do it."

Essie says, "Do you really think so?"

"I do think so. It is an honor, Essie. I wish that I were there to help you."

Essie decides, "I can do all things through Christ which strengthened me. Philippians 4:13." I send my love to the family and hang up. Whew! That's one obstacle out of the way without any effort at all on my part.

Cuba is on my mind, but I don't know a lot about it. The library will hold the answer so I stroll across campus to the library that's been standing since the 1800s. Using both hands to shove open the heavy doors, I head for the reference librarian.

She smiles and says, "How may I help you?"

"I want to know more about Cuba—where things are located."

"You mean like, a map?"

"Yes, I'm sorry. That's what I mean."

"Our atlas stand is directly behind you, in the reference section. I suggest you start with an atlas that contains political maps that show county, state, and national boundaries. Those should be in the top drawer."

Pulling out the top drawer, I choose an atlas, place it on the slanted top of the atlas stand, and open it to the Caribbean. Of course, Florida's Key West and Havana are very close together. If I pursued this wild idea of getting into Cuba at all that may not be the best way to do it. Havana is where all the action is. I'd be really conspicuous there.

I move my index finger over the map of Cuba. It's divided into different provinces; that's not helpful. I broaden my search outside Cuba and see that Haiti is not too far from Cuba's shores. Neither is Jamaica *Jamaica? My gosh! Luke is going to Montego Bay in less than two weeks!*

I make another trip to see Father Walsh. "Father, can you send a message in the diplomatic pouch for me? I need to send a message to Cuba. It has to go out today."

"The embassy folks will let me do that, Ellen. What do I send? I assume it's going to James Baker who will get it to David?"

"Yes. Please tell him that I can be in Montego Bay, Jamaica, from April eighteenth to the twenty-second. Ask him if there's any way I could help in getting Zia out. Jamaica is so close to the eastern end of Cuba." I look at Father Walsh, trying to read his expression. "I know it sounds crazy, Father, but it just so happens that the broadcast kids are going to Montego Bay on those dates. Luke asked me to go. Don't you just see the hand of God in this? Here," I say, picking up a pen on his desk. "I'll write it all out."

"Well, Ellen. I'll send your message," he says. "Then, we'll see what happens. I'll call you as soon as I get a reply."

"I don't know what I'd do without you, Father. Thank you so much."

You know it's really hard; just David, Father Walsh, and I are dealing with this, but we can do it. I know we can do it. Still, truth is, I'm worried sick.

Father Walsh calls the day after we send a message out. An answer from David is in the daily pouch. He is excited about the possibilities with Montego Bay. Many of his sugar cane plantations were in Oriente on the eastern end of Cuba just across the water from Montego Bay. Even though Castro owns the plantations once belonging to David, there are still families in the area loyal to David.

David writes, "Paco and Luisa Perez work on a plantation that's not too far from Santiago, Cuba. Paco has a brother who is a fisherman in Montego Bay. Get to Montego Bay and Paco's brother, Manuel, will take you to Cuba then to Paco and Luisa."

"I will get Zia to Paco's," he has written. "I really have to be careful. I got Zia out of La Cabaña, but she is so fragile. The whole situation is fragile. Castro is watching me closely. I may not be able to bring her myself. I just don't know. Let's plan to meet at Paco and Luisa's on April 20; I think that will work."

I show the letter to Father Walsh. He crosses himself. "Ellen, are you sure about this?" he asks. "So many bad things can happen."

"It's really moving fast, Father, but yes. I am sure that I want to do this. I have to make it happen. Aunt Zia needs me."

"Let's think about basics. You have to buy a round-trip ticket to Montego Bay. Find out what flights Luke is taking—I'm going to buy a ticket for you on the same flight. We'll go to the airport tomorrow to arrange it all. Do you have a passport?"

"Yes, Father."

"Good. That's all you need. You won't need a visa. Be thankful for that. Assuming Zia's passport is current, she'll be OK, too. That's all the paperwork she'll need. Oh, yes. She's got to have a ticket to fly from Jamaica to Miami. I'm paying for that as well."

"Father, this is not your fight. How can you buy all these tickets?"

Father Walsh smiles, "Ellen, David Foca is a wealthy man despite Castro. He'll pay me back, and eventually I'm going to ask him for a contribution to the Pedro Pan movement. I think he'll be happy to do that without any complaint at all if we can make this happen. Just think how much better he'll feel with his beloved Zia safe. He may never leave Cuba because of Carlota, but thanks to you at least he won't have to worry about Zia and Julio."

"Father, you really are a lifesaver to me. I'm going to talk to Luke, and I'll be back in touch today or tomorrow. Bless you for what you have done and are doing for our family and for so many others."

I find Luke in the broadcasting room. He is in the middle of writing a script for the evening news. He is so totally involved in what he is doing that he doesn't see me walk up.

"Hey, Luke the Legend."

"Cotton. I didn't know that you were there. What's happening?"

"I need to know the airline and flight number for your trip to Montego Bay."

"And why do you need that?"

"Because I wanna go with ya. Sounds like a wonderful trip." I smile my best smile.

"That is the best news I've heard all week. That's wonderful, Cotton."

"There's one thing, Luke. There will be a couple days that I won't be with you. You can't ask me about it. I'll tell you on the trip home but not before."

"That's really mysterious, lady. If you go, I'm gonna feel responsible. I can't just let you take off."

"You are going to have to do just that, Luke. It's something *Trust* that I've got to do. Do you trust me?"

"You, who lives with a mantra of *Truth and Honor?*" He

smiles. "Of course, I trust you."

"Well, just trust me now. You got those flight numbers?"

"Let's go get them. They are in my dorm room."

"By the way, where are we staying?"

"The Bay Roc. Ellen, it's gonna be fabulous. It's right on the beach, and our crowd is in a cottage. Plenty of room for everybody."

"As long as I have my own bed, I'm happy."

Well, well. Luke the Legend seems to be blushing.

The next day Father Walsh and I go to the airport to buy tickets for a flight from Miami to Montego Bay and two return flights. Before I know it, I'm holding the tickets in my hand. *Ellen, this is real. What are you doing?* I think.

I write a brief note to David that Father Walsh will send ahead of me. I tell him Father Walsh bought plane tickets for me and Aunt Zia. I tell him we will be staying at Bay Roc in Montego Bay.

Another letter from David comes in the diplomatic pouch. Father Walsh calls me to come to the welfare bureau so we can talk. The letter confirms all the details. Everything is falling into place. Paco and Luisa have agreed to help. In his letter, David goes on to prepare me for what I'm going to see when I get to Cuba.

Manuel will land the boat on plantation land, and we'll walk to Paco's. Paco is one of the few workers living in a house. Most live in dorms. Fortunately, his house is on the outskirts of the ingenio, the complex that includes offices, the sugar mill, a sugar refinery, a town, and sugar fields. I'll only see this from a distance while staying inside Paco and Luisa's home.

He goes on to say that if anyone does see me, I'm to say that I'm with the Literacy Brigade, a volunteer from Jamaica. Britain has control over Jamaica, and it is feasible that some people on the island will help with the Brigade. After all, volunteers come to Cuba from several countries to help. If that happens, I sure hope my high school and college Spanish will get me by.

Rescue Plans

David still doesn't know how he will get Zia to Paco's. He's going to bring her if he can. It all depends on Castro and any demands he might make on David that day. He will send her if he can't bring her on his own.

I'll be in Manuel's hands. Manuel will be selling fish right on the beach in front of the hotel in the late afternoon. It will be my job to find him as other fishermen will be there as well. He will take me to Cuba during the night. I'm to contact him in the afternoon, and he will tell me where to meet him that night.

Rescue Plans

Before I know it, it is the fifteenth of April and, if things aren't complicated enough, something is happening in Cuba. I don't know if or how this might affect my getting into Cuba. It seems that an attempt has been made to destroy Castro's Cuban Air Force. B26 bombers have strafed the military bases where planes were stored. News reports indicate that all but six planes in Castro's Air Force were destroyed. Some reporters speculate it may be a revolt by Castro's own men.

Castro's Air Force destroyed

Two days later, things are worse. We fly to Jamaica tomorrow morning. Today, we are receiving sketchy reports that Cuban exiles are landing in the southern part of Cuba, an area called the Bay of Pigs. On the eighteenth, Luke picks me up at the dorm, and we load the car for the trip to the airport.

I'm putting my luggage in the trunk when Luke grabs me

by the shoulders and turns me to face him. Without warning, he picks me up and turns round and round. He's swinging me through the air as fast as he can.

When I can catch my breath, I ask "Luke, you doofus. Why did you do that?"

"Because I'm happy. I can already see you on the beach, Cotton. Ya have a bikini?"

"Sure Luke. Actually, I have two." I laugh at the expression on his face.

"Well, I guess you'll be some dish. Can't wait to share a beach with you."

"Yeah? Well, I'm looking forward to being on the beach with Luke the Legend." I smile as I lean in to kiss him.

We meet the other broadcasting students at the airport and board our flight at 7:00 p.m. Jamaica is one hour behind us, so we'll land a little after 7:00 p.m. Jamaica time. Cool, huh?

On the flight over, I read about Jamaica. It's under British rule, but there is a strong connection to Africa throughout the country. Jamaica was part of the infamous slave triangle. Slaves were purchased in Africa and smuggled into the country with foods brought from Europe. These slaves were sold in Jamaica for goods which were traded to Europe. Jamaica ended slavery in 1838, thank goodness, but it's a big part of the island's history.

We fly into Donald Sangster International Airport at Montego Bay and are taken by shuttle to Bay Roc. I'm fascinated. It's so lush. I see trees everywhere and clear, clear water sparkling beneath the bright sun. We are driving on the left, and it is hard to get used to this. Plus, there are no stop lights, and no major highways I can see. It's an adventure, for sure.

Bay Roc is something. The beach with shimmering, brilliantly white sand is bordered by turquoise water on one side and trees on the other. There's a pool right by the ocean. You can almost step from one to the other. Black and white umbrellas dot the beach. It's not like any place I've been before.

After we settle in, we have a late dinner at the hotel. Then we walk down to the beach. It's just like David said it would be. Fishermen are on the beach selling fish. Tourists and locals are cooking fish right on the beach. The smell of wood burning and fish cooking mixes with the salty smell of the ocean. It is exotic. I don't have to worry about Manuel until tomorrow. I can almost forget why I'm here. I put my arm around Luke's waist, and we walk.

When I come in the cottage kitchen the next morning, the broadcast kids are watching the news and talking about Cuba. It seems that the Bay of Pigs landing was an utter disaster for the Cuban exiles landing with American transportation and weapons. Those six planes in Castro's Air Force left undestroyed wreaked havoc with the landing force. Some among our group are arguing about Kennedy and the fact he refused to send U.S. air support.

One newscast reports that the Bay of Pigs landing was scheduled to occur simultaneously with a revolt in Cuba. Castro was to be assassinated during the revolt. I freeze. The assassination attempt they are talking about is the one planned by Jorge and the others captured in Zia's neighborhood. I hope she never realizes the result of her panicked run from the militia.

Luke says, "Hey, news junkies. We're in Jamaica. Let's get out on the beach. Forget Cuba!"

Easier said than done, Luke. Easier said than done.

I love the beach. I stand at the water's edge and throw my arms high in the sky. I just stand there like that smelling the salt and listening to the waves. I love the way I can squeeze the sand between my toes. Most of all, I love how the tide comes in and washes it all away. It's glorious.

I alternate between lying on the beach beside Luke and going in the water. I've snorkeled at the Gulf in Alabama before, so I am at ease doing that here. Underwater, I see small fish, some turtles, sting rays, and some cool coral. We make plans to roast fish on the shore tonight, and I remind Luke that I'm disappearing for a while. Actually, I'm disappearing tonight.

"Cotton, I don't understand this. You've never been to Jamaica before, and you're telling me that you're just going to disappear for a day or two. Who wouldn't think that's weird?"

"Luke, I know that it sounds like something out of a Hitchcock movie. Remember that I asked you to trust me? I'll explain everything on Saturday."

I can see that Luke is really disturbed. It's time to go get out of my bathing suit and get ready for dinner, so I walk back up to the cottage alone.

Four or five fishermen have their wooden fishing boats pulled up on the beach where they are selling fish. Part of our group is getting the fire ready while the rest of us talk to the fishermen. I hear one of the fishermen ask Luke's name.

"Me llamo Luke. ¿Como se llama?

"Me llamo Manuel."

I turn and stick out my hand to Manuel and smile, "Hi, Manuel. I'm Ellen."

When Luke turns to say something to one of the other kids, Manuel whispers, "Meet you right here at 2:00 a.m., Ellen."

The genuine smile on a brown, weathered face, and eyes

looking directly into mine, helped me relax. I didn't know how tightly I had been squeezing myself inside. I let go and just look at Manuel, nodding.

After everyone has gone to bed, I lie there thinking about how crazy this is. I think of everything that could go wrong. Was I wrong to not tell Luke? If I told him and ran into trouble, at least he would know where I am. I don't want him involved in this. I really don't. I toss and turn.

It's almost 2:00 a.m. on the twentieth of April. I put on black pants and a top. *Maybe they'll cast me in the sequel to* The Cat Burglar, I think. I tiptoe out of my room and look in on Luke. He's sprawled out on his stomach, snoring up a storm. I want to brush that hair out of his eyes and kiss him. I don't.

I walk down to the beach. I'm calm and in a good place. Manuel is there waiting for me. I climb into the boat—it's not the fishing boat that Manuel had earlier but a speedboat. I guess getting to Cuba in the smaller boat would take forever. Manuel points to the tarp on the bottom of the boat. I'm to climb under the tarp if we see another boat. It's going to take all night to get to Cuba, so I settle in and try to remain calm. Two hours into our trip I see lights off to my right. I watch as they get closer and closer, and slide under the tarp.

I hear, "Hola. Manuel, ¿Es tu?"

Manuel shouts across the water, "Diego. Viejo. Tu ere demasiado viejo para ser tan tarde."

"Nunca se es demasiado viejo, Manuel. Nunca."

"Tener cuidado, mi amigo."

I hear the sound of the motor fade away in the distance. When I hear nothing, I feel Manuel tap on the tarp and climb out from under with a wide grin. He smiles back.

At dawn, I see the shore in front of us. It's not good that we didn't land in the dark, but there's no help for it. I step onto Cuban soil and am immediately surrounded by dense foliage. There's a smooth path that's been worn away by hundreds of feet that have passed this way before me. According to Manuel, this path leads to Paco and Luisa's house. He motions to me to take off my shoes. We move smoothly along the path careful not to touch the surrounding bushes or make any noise.

I see a small house up ahead, and Manuel nods—that's where we're going. The house is made of boards painted lime green. There's a thatched roof attached to the front of the house that slopes down. It looks like it's about to fall as it is held up by uneven and thin wooden supports. Even though it's early in the morning, I see smoke coming from the lone chimney. Paco and Luisa are awake.

Manuel knocks on the door. The door opens and standing in front of us is Manuel's duplicate. Paco has the same brown, weathered face and the same huge smile. Luisa comes to the door as well. She's wiping her hands on an apron and scolding Paco for not inviting us in. She's missing a front tooth. Her hair is pulled up in a bun, and the apron covers what appears to be a rather short, rotund body. Luisa pats my cheeks then pulls me inside. She insists that I sit down at the one table in the room. She's gonna feed us breakfast. I immediately feel comfortable.

After breakfast, Manuel says his goodbyes. He promises to be back to pick me up by midnight two days from now. I'm left with Paco and Luisa. They say that they have to go work in the fields and I should stay out of sight in the house. *No problem there*, I think. I'm scared.

I wait all day listening to shouts from the workers and the clatter made by the machines extracting the juice from the sugar cane. Once in a while, I hear laughter from children.

I keep expecting Zia. I still don't know who is bringing her. I console myself by telling myself she won't come until it's dark. I try to visualize what she'll look like—what she'll be like—after her terrible experience.

Finally, it's dusk. Paco and Luisa come in from the fields, and Luisa immediately starts dinner. She serves rice and beans with fried plantains. It's fabulous. Luisa smiles at the way I wolf down my food. I can tell that she's flattered. Essie would be horrified to see me eat like this.

After dinner, we go to bed. I lie awake on my thin palette on the floor. I keep listening for Zia. Manuel is picking me up tomorrow night at midnight. I have to have Zia with me! I just have to.

I awake to hear Paco open the front door. It's still dark. I hear him whispering with someone and get up to see who's there. First, I see David. He's holding Zia in his arms. He's holding a much older Zia who seems to have no life left in her. I run and grab them both, holding on for dear life. Zia is here!

We sit around the table, drink strong coffee, and talk until daylight. I tell David what I know about Julio. I tell him all the news from Callander, including Essie's role in Dad and Amanda's wedding. I tell him about Luke. Zia sits and drinks coffee, but says nothing.

David talks about Havana and the Bay of Pigs. He heard that Castro placed women and children in an armaments building to deter bombing there. He adds that, if the people of Havana had revolted at the same time as the Bay of Pigs landing, the outcome might have been different. It was an embarrassment for the CIA-backed Cuban exiles. Over 1,100 soldiers from the invading force were imprisoned in La Cabaña. David left a Havana immersed in chaos.

While David is talking, Zia sits beside him, gripping his hand. David looks at me and says, "I've got to go, Ellen. This is killing me, but I've got to go. We're all in danger."

He turns to Zia. "Love of my life, you are going with Ellen tonight. She is taking you to Callander. I will be with you as soon as I can leave Cuba." He puts his large hand behind her head and moves her to his body. Her head is on his shoulder. Her eyes are closed, and I see tears slowly making their way down her cheeks. This is the first reaction I've seen from her.

David kisses Zia, then rises to leave. He turns to me. "Ellen, I know how much danger you and Zia are in and how very brave you are to come to Cuba. Please get word to me as soon as you are in Montego Bay. Take care of her!"

David walks out the door, and I sit there by Zia. I start telling her about Callander—every little thing that I can think of even though I'm repeating everything I said to David earlier. I see reaction in her eyes when I tell her about Dad and Amanda. I spend the day holding her and talking to her.

Finally, it is the twenty-second of April. As promised, Manuel comes at midnight. I hug Luisa and then Paco. Luisa gives us empanadas to eat on the trip back to Montego Bay. How can I possibly thank them for all they have done?

We follow the same smooth path back to Manuel's boat. I try to convey to Zia that she must be quiet. When we get to the boat, I expect a struggle with Zia, but she quietly climbs onto the boat and sits down. She has always surprised me. Today is no different.

The long trip back to Montego Bay is uneventful. No red lights in the distance and no contact with another boat. When we pull up on the shore of Montego Bay, I tremble. So many things could have gone wrong. But they didn't. Zia cannot be harmed by Castro now. Paco and Luisa can. David can. But Zia is safe.

I look at Manuel's weathered face. He smiles. I smile back and walk over to him to shake his hand. I tell him that if he ever needs my help, he's got it.

Zia and I walk into the cottage where all the broadcasting kids are packing and talking loudly. As we stand in the door, everyone stops talking. I'm sure that Zia and I are a bedraggled sight. "Good morning," I say. "I'd like for you all to meet my Aunt Zia."

Everyone freezes and stares at us like we have two heads. Finally, Luke walks over and takes Aunt Zia's hand in his. He smiles and says, "Welcome back, Aunt Zia." She actually smiles at him. He then turns to me and says, "Cotton", then walks into his bedroom so I follow, whispering to Aunt Zia that I will be right back.

"Luke, we had to bring her out of Cuba. I had to go get her. You see the shape she's in."

"Cotton, we'd better take this to the beach."

We walk out through the main room of the house. I see that the broadcast girls are taking care of Zia. We walk down the steps of the cottage onto the beach.

"OK, Ellen. I want to hear it all."

I start with the very first letter from David that tells about Aunt Zia in La Cabaña. I end with Manuel bringing us from Cuba to Montego Bay. "I didn't want to involve you, Luke. I care too much to want to hurt you in any way. The ending of this tale could have been tragic. But, hey, it wasn't. Everything's good."

Luke grabs me, hugs me, and kisses me deeply. I stand in his arms until one of the broadcasting students yells, "Get a move on, you two. We have an 11:00 a.m. flight!"

Our flight back to Miami is uneventful. I try to explain everything that has happened from the Miami side of things. Zia listens. Before we left, I made two calls from the airport—one to Ann and one to Father Walsh. Father Walsh will get word back to David that the trip out was a success. Both Ann and Father Walsh insist on meeting us at the airport.

A short while later, once again, we are on American soil. I look at Zia. She seems interested in what's happening around her. Father Walsh and Ann are waiting at baggage claim. I make the introductions. "Aunt Zia, this is my roommate, Ann, and this is Father Walsh who helped us get Julio out of Cuba."

I see the well-bred, charming lady is still inside Zia although she is struggling to surface. She takes Father's hand saying slowly and deliberately, "Father, we owe you for Julio's life and, it seems, for mine as well. David and I thank you."

To Ann she actually says, "And you are the young lady that taught my niece to twist?" Her eyes light up the slightest bit.

Ann laughs and replies, "Guilty."

Father Walsh has arranged a room for Zia and me at the welfare bureau. He thought Zia would prefer this to a dorm, where there's little, if any, privacy. I walk over to get my suitcase off the baggage carousel but Luke leans across me and grabs my suitcase instead. I look into his eyes.

"Luke, I didn't just go to Montego Bay with you because it would give me access to Zia. I will go with you anywhere." I smile and add, "If I have money to buy a ticket."

He smiles back. "Where do you go from here, Cotton? You're gonna call your Dad, I guess. It's hard to believe no one knew about this. Can I help with anything?"

"Well, you can come by the welfare bureau tonight if you'd like. I'd love for you to be there. Don't understand why, but that's the way it is, I guess."

"OK, Cotton. I'll see you tonight. By the way, you are one ʔutsy woman." He doesn't tell me he loves me. He's only done t once. I know he won't say it again until I say it.

ʌunt Zia and I settle in at the welfare bureau then I call Dad. 't's Ellen. I think you need to come to Miami right away."

Dictator Foiled!

Rescue successful.

Chapter Eighteen: May 1961

The news from (Callander) is good. Essie is in the throes of planning how to decorate the plantation house for the wedding; Amanda is buying her trousseau, and Aunt Zia is coming back to life. She has spoken to me on the phone several times. Dad reports that Zia calls Julio several times a week and walks up to Jonas Stockman's grave every day. I often think of how life would have been had she stayed in Havana and shudder. *Normalcy + Tradition*

As for me, I'm beginning to cram for finals and packing for *Home* Colorado Springs. I fly out this Friday. I've talked to Jo Jo several times. He's constantly listing all the places he wants to take me.

Luke is not happy about this trip, and he insists that he take me to the airport Friday morning. He checks my luggage and waits with me until my flight is called. When we hear my flight number, we stand. Luke pulls me to him.

"Don't forget where you belong, Cotton." He kisses me on the forehead and walks away.

I have plenty of time to think on the flight but made no life *Home ?* decisions by the time the wheels are down. Jo Jo is waiting for me at the airport. This handsome soldier represents (home) to me. He hasn't changed.

He laughs. "Ellen, I can't believe that you're here! I can't wait to show you Colorado."

"It sounds pretty wonderful from what you've told me,"

"Let's go over to visitor's lodging and get you checked

in. We'll start right away with everything that's right here on campus. Tomorrow morning we'll see off-campus stuff and get you back in time to get ready for the dance."

Our first stop on campus is the chapel which is a work in progress. Jo Jo says, "The chapel is part of what we call the Cadet Area. All the main buildings are set around a large square pavilion called the Terrazzo. For sure, the chapel is the most outstanding."

The chapel is made of aluminum, glass, and steel. "When it is finished, it will be 150 feet high," says Jo Jo.

I see the beginnings of seventeen spires and can only imagine how impressive the chapel will be when it's finished.

"All faiths worship here, Jo Jo?"

Religious Tolerance

"As far as I know. There are separate chapels for Protestant, Catholic, Jewish, and Buddhist faiths. I think there are some all-faith worship rooms as well."

"It's very modern—sleek. It's sleek."

"Let me show you the other buildings. That's my dorm." Jo Jo indicates by tilting his head to the left. "It's called Vandenberg Hall." It looks like three boxes stacked on top of each other with the smallest box at the bottom and the largest box on the top. Lots of glass and aluminum.

I look across the grass and the brown, grainy Terrazzo to a less impressive building. "And that building?"

"This is where my classes are held—Fairchild Hall. Come on. Let's walk across the Terrazzo."

After the touring the Cadet Area, we're glad to go get a Coke and catch up. Jo Jo is just waiting for all the Callander news. He's surprised Dad is getting married, and, of course, he wants to know about all the sharecroppers and their families. I save the story of Aunt Zia for tomorrow.

We start off early the next morning for Pikes Peak. On the way, I tell the story of rescuing Aunt Zia. I don't leave anything out. I tell Jo Jo about Father Walsh and how he helped me; about Luke and the broadcast kids; and how we went to Montego Bay. I tell him about Manuel and the trip to Cuba and back.

Jo Jo says, "Ellen, this Luke. . . He seems to be an important part of this story."

Truth and Honor I look Jo Jo straight in the eye and say, "He's important." Silence. We leave the subject there and go on to talk about Jo Jo's life as a cadet.

Living in Alabama and Florida, I've never seen anything like the scenery on the Pikes Peak Highway. We start up the mountain at around 7,400 feet and climb to over 14,000 feet. It's jaw-dropping beautiful—like going above the clouds. On the way back down the mountain, Jo Jo talks about where he's going in life. He will be commissioned as an officer in the Air Force and is interested in the Air Police. He knows about my interest in broadcast journalism, so I tell him about my experiences at the J-school.

Our next stop is the Broadmoor for lunch. The Broadmoor is posh, so posh that in one area, there's an authentic pub shipped over from England. It's pink and kinda fits with the landscape. Jo Jo and I eat at one of the outside restaurants.

Then on to the Garden of the Gods to see the huge, red sandstone rocks—every shape and size imaginable. What fascinates me is how the rocks are balanced—one on top of another, looking as though a tiny push will send them tumbling. We hike until Jo Jo says it's time to turn back and go get dressed for the big night.

While in the visitor's center getting dressed in my room, I think about how comfortable I am with Jo Jo. What a fun day we've had. I have a new dress for the occasion. It's white and strapless, falling full length to the floor and I'm wearing a hoop skirt under it. I wear dangling pearl earrings and elbow-length, white gloves with tiny buttons. How wonderful to feel so pretty!

When Jo Jo picks me up, he looks at me and whistles. I twirl around then curtsy. He laughs and tucks my arm under his. We're ready to dance.

The dance is already under way when we get there. We start with a slow dance to *Smoke Gets In Your Eyes*. It's dreamy. The next song is Chubby Checker's *Twist*.

Jo Jo asks, "Can you twist?"

I say, "You just try to keep up with me!"

We laugh through the entire dance. What a blast! The dance is over too soon with the last song being *In the Still of the Night*. When the dance is over, we stand in the middle of the floor. Jo Jo says, "Ellen, I think you've got something going with Luke. I understand that. You just remember that I'm here for you—always will be."

I stand on tiptoes and kiss Jo Jo's forehead. "Thank you, Jo Jo. I won't forget."

The next morning I'm on the flight back to Miami. I expect to see Luke waiting at the airport when we land. Luke's not there; Ann is. She wants to know all about the trip, and we talk all the way to campus.

"Have you seen Luke?"

Ann replies, "Nope. I've seen a couple of the broadcast

crew, and they say he's cruisin' for a bruisin'. No one wants to be around him."

Oops! I think I'd better unpack and go find him. I find him in the studio, talking to some broadcast girls. I walk up and put my arm around his waist. He smiles down at me. "Glad you're home, Cotton."

I'm glad, too.

Luke, Callander, and Zia take a back seat to finals. Ann and I think that if we stay up all night studying the night before a final it will help. Two nights of staying up all night changes our minds about that theory. Last night we slept the sleep of the dead and woke up feeling much better about today's finals. This is our last day. Thank gosh. My last final of the day is art class. I actually look forward to it.

After the art final, which included creating a painting—trying to capture what makes a tree a tree, I say goodbye to Ann and drag my luggage down the stairs. Luke is taking me to the airport. He's not talking very much.

On the way to the airport, *See You In September* is playing on the radio. How appropriate. All of a sudden, Luke throws his head back and starts singing along with The Tempos. He glances at me and grins. Luke grabs most of my luggage and walks me to the gate. I have really mixed feelings about leaving him. He's interning at a local Miami television station instead of going home for the summer. At least I'll know where to find him.

When we get to the gate, Luke puts my luggage down and hugs me. I feel the beginnings of his beard on my cheeks and smell the peppermint on his breath. I feel so at home with him. I squeeze him and kiss him, then I get on the plane. I'm not gonna cry. I am not going to cry. On the flight home, I think about all that has happened this school year—meeting Amanda, getting Julio to the United States, rescuing Zia, and, maybe, loving Luke?

I think of Luella and her predictions for me.

I will be an advocate for the beauty.

I will foil a dictator.

I will find the soldier.

Certainly, I was an advocate for Neta Levy, and you know, I guess I helped throw a wrench in the dictator's works as well, because Julio will never be indoctrinated in Marxism and communism. Zia is free and out of Castro's reach. It seems Luella has done it again. We'll have to wait and see about the soldier, but I'm becoming a believer in Luella and her predictions.

Foiling dictator

Sounds cheesy, but coming home is like wrapping a warm blanket around myself. Dad picked me up at the Mobile airport, and we have plenty of time to talk about the plantation, Zia, and, of course, the wedding.

When we get home from the airport I find Essie is up at the plantation house, but Zia is there, standing on the steps and waiting to greet me, looking like her old self. We hug for the longest time. I look in her eyes and see shadows of all the terror she lived through in Havana. Despite what I see reflected in her eyes, she really looks wonderful. We spend the day catching up.

The next morning I wake in my old room. I lie in bed and tick off all the exciting things happening today. Julio is coming to Callander this afternoon, and the wedding rehearsal is tonight. I have to find some time to go visit Jonas. Too much excitement!

Tradition

I go down for breakfast. Dad has left to run errands, but Aunt Zia and Essie are at the kitchen table. Essie says, "Come on, child. We're having French toast." Essie insists on fixing a plate of toast for me before eating her own. I smother the toast in syrup, cut a bite, and put it in my mouth. *Yum!* I've really missed this.

Zia says, "Ellen, Essie has a secret. I'll bet you can wheedle it out of her."

"Oh, really? Come on Essie. Tell me what it is."

"OK," Essie says. "But you can't tell!"

"All right, all right. I promise!"

Essie says, "Do you remember that the plantation house at one time had a functioning ballroom? And that the room is still there? It's the right wing of the house. It's been used for storage since the early 1900s. No one ever goes in there."

"A ballroom? How romantic."

Zia says, "Ellen, Essie has reclaimed that ballroom. She's had everyone on the plantation helping her get rid of the junk stored there. Essie, tell Ellen what you found when the dust settled."

"Ellen, you won't believe this! We found six-foot wrought iron candle holders with glass chimneys. There are enough to place between each of the windows of the ballroom. They are made so that greenery can be tucked around the base of the chimney."

"Oh, that sounds fabulous! What else?"

"The ceiling is fourteen feet high and includes three large chandelier medallions. The windows stretch almost floor to ceiling. There are two-foot wooden panels below each window that appear to be a part of the wall but open back on hinges to create enough space to use the windows as doors. These will be opened for the reception—but not a moment before."

"And what else, Essie?"

"Can't tell you. I want you to be surprised along with everyone else."

"Essie, you are amazing. What talent!"

I smother a chuckle as Essie says, "No one lights a lamp and hides it in a clay jar or puts it under a bed. Luke 8:16."

Zia and I agree to visit Jonas Stockman's grave. We've spent many hours together at his grave in the past making up stories about his life and speculating about why *Truth and Honor* are engraved on his tombstone. It's wonderful to be standing with Aunt Zia at Jonas' grave again. I realize that only one month ago Aunt Zia was still in Cuba. One month ago I was packing for a trip to Montego Bay with Luke the Legend.

She opens up and talks to me about being in La Cabaña. She talks about what it was like to hear music and everyday life going on over the wall while on her side, she was forced to watch while Che Guevara's men marched the conspirators out and shot them one by one.

"I couldn't turn my eyes away, Ellen. I watched until the last man went down. The image is engraved on my retina. It won't go away." She looks down for a moment, then looks me straight in the eyes. "Ellen, you were so brave to come to Cuba after me. I'll never forget what you did for me."

"Are you able to communicate with David?"

"Nothing from David. I've heard no news from Cuba at all. I worry every day Castro will punish David. Castro has to know that David helped me leave the country."

"Zia, David is important to Castro. He won't harm him."

"Well, I'll pray that that is true. We won't mention this to Julio. Now tell me about this Luke fellow."

I talk to Zia about Luke and my visit to Jo Jo in Colorado. I tell her all about the dance and the sights at Colorado Springs, and I tell her about the folks at the J-building. I even tell her about my trip to The Bowl with Luke.

"Well, Ellen, my girl. I think that you're in love. I have to tell you that I like him." She smiled, then turned to walk back toward the house, leaving me alone with Jonas. I realize after she walked away that she didn't say who she thought I loved. Luke? Or Jo Jo?

When I return from the grave, Julio is here. Gosh, he looks so much older and mature in his uniform. We all sit around the kitchen table and talk. Marion Military Institute is out for the summer, so Julio will be home, here at Callander. If I know Julio, he'll be following Grandfather and the sharecroppers all summer. He loves everything that's involved in running Callander.

We dress for the rehearsal and ride up to the plantation house. Mother's sister, Aunt Eleanor, is directing the wedding. She has opened up the president's home on campus for the rehearsal dinner.

The wedding will take place on the front porch of the plantation house, and the guests will watch the exchanging of vows from the lawn. Dad and preacher Willis are standing on the front porch. Zia is the matron of honor and I am the maid of honor. The ushers, Zia, and I walk around from the side porches and position ourselves on the front porch. The double front doors are closed.

A baby grand piano has been rolled out onto the porch. As the wedding march begins, two ushers will simultaneously open the double doors, and Amanda will walk through them. Since this is a rehearsal, Essie is filling in for the bride. There's a lot of teasing and laughter about Essie's role. She takes it all in stride.

After the rehearsal, we ride into town to Aunt Eleanor's home at Rose Hall for dinner. I take a quick stroll through the huge rose garden in the rear of the house. I have to think of Ann Carson and her sad story. Roses are planted in front of the house, too, blooming like crazy behind a row of boxwoods. The smell is delicious. When I have a home, I want tons of roses.

The rehearsal dinner is in typical Aunt Eleanor style. Not only is the dinner amazing, but the lights are dimmed, and the center of the long dining table is lined with candles. I enjoy watching Dad and Amanda. It's obvious they really care for each other. It has been an amazing day. I'll keep it in my memory and pull it out from time to time to experience it all over again. Tomorrow will be even better.

May 20—the wedding day is here. The day is a blur until I walk out on the porch at the plantation house in my fern green, floor-length dress. Zia follows me out onto the porch and stands beside me. Dad is on the other side of the porch with his entourage. I wink at him.

We are waiting for the wedding march to begin. I scan the crowd standing on the lawn below. There are so many old friends, all here to watch Dad and Amanda marry and to wish them well. But wait! I can hardly believe what I'm seeing. Luke is standing at the back of the crowd!

Zia sees that I've noticed Luke. She takes my hand, squeezes it, and leans over to whisper, "I invited him, Ellen."

After the wedding, I stand on the porch and wait for Luke to walk up the front walk. You know, I don't think I've ever seen him in a suit and tie. When he reaches me, he doesn't touch me. He looks into my eyes and smiles.

"Surprised?" he asks.

"Thrilled," I answer.

Before we can talk further, Preacher Willis invites the guests into the ballroom for the reception. I can hardly describe what Essie has accomplished. The windows to the ballroom stand open. The first thing I notice as we walk inside are the wrought iron candle holders. The glass chimneys sparkle around the tapers lit inside. Essie has added magnolia blossoms in full bloom with their shiny greenery to the base of each chimney. They line the ballroom—so simple but so classy.

Three huge chandeliers hang from the medallions in the ceiling, and you can see your reflection in the polished heart pine floor. Essie has an orchestra stationed at the far end of the room. They play *Moon River* as Dad and Amanda walk onto the floor for the first dance.

Breaking protocol, Dad dances the second dance with Essie while Julio dances with Amanda. My throat tightens as I watch them. They are so beautiful. I turn and walk onto the dance floor with Luke.

The orchestra is playing *When I Fall in Love*. I look up at Luke and remind myself this is not a dream. I really am dancing with him at Dad and Amanda's wedding. He smiles. I smile back, and say the words I wanted to be sure of before I said them. . . "I love you."

Love — Luke

Part three
Ellen finds the
Soldier

Chapter Nineteen: June 1961

I'm standing at Jonas Stockman's grave. I think about all the stories that Aunt Zia and I have made up about Jonas and his life. It would be so cool to know the real Jonas Stockman. *Well, why not? Why can't I try to find out who he was?* There's got to be a record of him somewhere.

I lay a stone on Jonas' grave and head home. Dad and Amanda are still on their honeymoon. It's just Essie, Aunt Zia, and me for now, and Essie'll be moving back to town soon. We talk for a while before I head up to bed.

The next morning, I put on my old chenille robe and slowly make my way downstairs. Aunt Zia is still asleep, but Essie is up and fixing breakfast, French toast again. She always heats the syrup with butter. I love Essie's cooking.

"Ellen, you need to eat in a hurry. David Henry wants to see you at the plantation house."

"Ya know what he wants?"

"No, ma'am. He just said that he has a project for you."

I usually like to eat my French toast slowly, swirling the toast in the warm syrup while talking with Essie. Not this morning. I eat in a hurry and rush upstairs to put on pedal pushers and a blouse. I slip on my white canvas shoes, run a brush through my hair, and add a smear of lipstick. I yell as I'm going out the door, "Essie, I'll see ya later. I'll be at the plantation house."

I cross the wide porch of the plantation house, open the looming doors and step into the wide hall. I smell a mixture of coffee, maybe cinnamon rolls, and the lemon oil that's been used for years on the Callander antiques.

"Ellen, is that you?" questions Grandfather. "Come on in the study."

I stop in the door to the study. Just look at all those books. I used to love to pick one and crawl in the kneehole of grandfather's desk to read.

"Morning, Ellen. Come sit. I have a proposition for you, young lady."

"OK, I'm really curious. What sorta proposition?"

"You have some time before you go back to college. How would you like to earn some spending money by clearing out the attic here at the house?"

I'm not wild about the attic, but I sure could use the money. "How much are you going to pay me?"

Grandfather laughs and says, "Well, I doubt if you can get everything done before you go back to school. How about fifty dollars for cleaning out everything but the trunks? You can finish the trunks next summer."

"Yes, sir, I can do that. I bet you want me to start this morning. I'll just go up and eyeball the attic."

Down the wide hall is the one door in the house that's always closed. I open it and peer up, my eyes following the narrow, wooden steps that lead to the attic. It's been ages since I've been up here. When I get to the top of the stairs and look around, I wonder what made me agree to do this.

In the attic, I see old Christmas trees, one of them fully decorated. I see a dressmaker's dummy, stacks of vinyl records, apple crates turned on their sides and filled with *National*

Geographic magazines. Look at all the lamps without shades and the stacks of suitcases. Some of the suitcases have stickers on them from Paris, London, and Venice.

There's an old iron bed piled high with quilts. I pick up the corner of one quilt that I remember. All those tiny stitches. Imagine the women who helped make these quilts. There's furniture too—end tables, chairs, beds, and dressers. They are all piled up on top of each other and look totally dejected. Somebody can use this furniture.

And, oh, look at the trunks! Rows of trunks. Now I'm interested. Who knows what kind of loot is in those trunks?

I walk back downstairs and ask Granddaddy, "Will you come up to the attic for just a minute?"

"Sure, Ellen. Be right there."

"OK, this is a thought. I want to keep the quilts, but is there anything else up here you wanna save?"

"Ellen, to me it's just junk. Get rid of everything except the quilts. We'll deal with the trunks later."

"How about this? You let me borrow a couple of men to haul most of this stuff to the empty cotton house. We'll let the plantation folks see if there's anything that they want. Roy at the antique shop might want to look at what's left. Then we'll haul the rest to the dump. One thing, I'll talk to Miss Brenda at the library to see if she wants the *National Geographics*."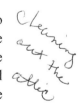

Cleaning out the attic

"That's a plan, child. Want the men to meet you here in the morning?"

"Yes, and thank you. I'll be here by eight-thirty."

I'm meeting Liz for lunch at the drugstore, so I drop back by the house to tell Essie where I'll be. I let the kitchen door bang as

I walk into the house.

"Essie, you won't believe this. Granddaddy is paying me to clean out the attic over there."

"Gee, Ellen. Do you need money that bad?"

"It's OK, Essie. I've got some free time. I'm here the whole summer. I've gotta have something to keep me busy. Right now I'm headed for Marshall. Meeting Liz for lunch. See ya later this afternoon."

As I drive to town, I'm thinking about Jonas. Maybe I'll ask Miss Brenda at the library how to go about researching him. Boy, would Zia be shocked if I could find out about the real Jonas.

Liz is already in a booth at the drugstore when I get there. I sit down and order my usual—grilled cheese and a Cherry Coke. I tell Liz all about the attic.

Liz says, "What an odd way to earn some bread!"

"Aw, come on Liz! Don't ya want to help me?"

"No way! I'm in summer school. Gotta study. By the way, guess who I saw in here yesterday? Jo Jo Reed. Did you know that he's home from basic training?"

"No, I didn't know. I haven't heard from him since I went out to Colorado Springs."

"Well, he's leaving in a couple of weeks for some place in Africa. You gotta see him before he leaves."

"Africa? Are you sure? Africa?"

"Yep. That's what he said."

"Weird. I'll go see him sometime today."

Liz and I finish lunch, and I head for the library. The Marshall library is my second home. Growing up, many of my Saturday afternoons were spent here. I open the door and immediately spot Miss Brenda.

"Ellen Jones. It's about time you came to visit," she says.

"Miss Brenda. It's so good to see you." I give her a big hug. "Actually, I'm on a mission. I'm cleaning out the attic at the plantation house and wonder if you could use some old copies of *National Geographic*."

"Well, Ellen. Every citizen in Marshall has tried to donate their old copies to the library. I'm afraid that the library is full of them."

"Oh. I didn't think about that. I do have another question. You know about the grave on Callander land that belongs to Revolutionary War soldier Jonas Stockman? How do I go about finding out about him?"

Miss Brenda asks, "Do you know anything at all about him?"

"Just that his grave says he was born in 1753 and died in 1829. Oh, and the phrase *Truth and Honor* is written on the grave."

"That's odd," Miss Brenda says. "Any graves that I've seen, and I've seen quite a few Revolutionary War soldiers' graves, don't have inscriptions on them. Wonder who put that there? And what it means?"

"That's part of the mystery, I guess. Any ideas on where to start looking for Jonas?"

"Well, we have census records on microfilm beginning in 1780. You know they take the census every ten years. Let's see what we can find." Miss Brenda turns and walks to the back of the library where a microfilm reader is set up on a large, wooden table. Metal cabinets at the end of the table hold the reels.

"Let's work backward, Ellen," she says. "He died in 1829, so let's look at the 1820 census." She threads the film in the machine and moves the knob, looking for the name Stockman. It's a blur on the screen until she stops in the general area where Stockman would be; she slowly scrolls through the names. She stops.

"Ellen. He's here. Look. He's here, Ellen."

I look over her shoulder and see that Jonas Stockman is listed as head of the family. We read down the page to see: *Number of free white males age 45 and up: 1.* The remaining thirty-one columns, some relating to wives, children, and slaves owned, are empty. So, Jonas owned no slaves and lived alone in 1820.

"Miss Brenda, I can't tell you how many times I've wondered who he was. Just this little bit makes him seem real."

"OK. Let's check the 1810 census." Miss Brenda removes the 1820 reel, replaces it in the cabinet and retrieves the 1810 reel. She threads it and begins to search. We see the name Stock followed by Stuman. No Jonas Stockman. Where was he before 1820?

I thank Miss Brenda and give her another hug. Time to go home. As I turn to leave, a slim, gray-haired lady, loaded down with library books, walks up to Miss Brenda. "Good afternoon, Miss Brenda. I've read all these books. Can you recommend some others?"

"Hello, Mrs. Maben. So good to see you. Do you know Ellen Jones?"

"I've seen you around town, but we've never met. You are as pretty as your mother," says Mrs. Maben. I stand as though my feet were nailed to the floor. I don't move, don't blink, and don't respond.

Miss Brenda, puzzled by my behavior, says, "Ellen, that's quite a compliment. Don't you think so?"

Gathering my manners, I say, "So nice to meet you, Mrs. Maben, and thank you so much for the compliment." I'm shaken and can't leave fast enough. I'm dragging all that guilt around about Mother and it intensifies when I see Mrs. Maben.

I decide to drive by the sharecroppers' houses to see if I can spot Jo Jo. Jo Jo's house is at the end of the row, and I see Mrs. Reed sitting on the porch. I park the car on the side of the road and walk over to Mrs. Reed.

"Mrs. Reed. So good to see you. Haven't seen you since the wedding."

"Oh, Ellen. That was sure some wedding. Everybody on the plantation was worthless the next day. And wasn't Miss Amanda a beautiful bride? We all think Mr. Jones is sure lucky."

"You know, Mrs. Reed, I think Dad is lucky, too."

"Is Jo Jo around? I hear he's home from basic training."

"He just walked over to the store. You'll find him there. Good to see you, Miss Ellen."

"Good to see you, too," I reply.

I get in the car and drive to the plantation store. Sure 'nuff. There's Jo Jo, standing on the front porch of the store.

I get out of my car and yell, "Jo Jo Reed, are you avoiding me?"

"Ellen Jones. You know better than that. I just got home yesterday morning."

Coming down the rickety steps and across the gravel, He picks me up and swings me. I laugh. "Jo Jo. It's so darn good to see you."

"Good to see you, pretty girl."

"What the heck is this about Africa? That's not true. You're not going there, are you?"

"Actually I am. I'm assigned to air police at Tripoli, Libya. That's in northern Africa, right on the Mediterranean."

"Should I worry about you?"

"Nah, not at all. I'll be having a ball learning a new culture and doing some scuba diving. Might even travel to Malta and Greece while I'm there."

"When are you leaving?"

"The fifth of July. I'm so glad I don't have to miss Mr. Callander's ribs on the Fourth!"

"Me, too. I'm thinking of asking Luke. Sure would like for you to meet him. You OK with that?"

"No, Ellen. I'll probably punch him out. . . Of course, I'm OK with it."

I hug Jo Jo. "You're the best, Jo Jo. You need to come to dinner before the Fourth. I'll talk to Essie. Do you care what night?"

"Nah. I don't care. Any night is good."

I turn and walk to the driver's side of the car. I open the door and yell over the roof to Jo Jo, "Hey, wait 'til you hear about my latest project."

Jo Jo grins. "I can hardly wait." He stresses the word *hardly*—

sarcastic devil.

I get in the car and drive home. When I walk into the kitchen, I smell Essie's meat loaf. "Hi, Essie. Meat loaf and peas for dinner?"

"Oh, hello Ellen. Yes, we're having meatloaf. By the way, Miss Brenda called from the library about forty minutes ago. Sounded excited. Maybe you can catch her."

I walk into the hall where is telephone is located. I'll bet it's something about Jonas. I pick up the heavy, black receiver and listen. For once, the Smiths up the road aren't on the party line. I dial the number for the library. I hear the phone ringing and, just when I'm about to give up, Miss Brenda answers.

"Miss Brenda. It's Ellen. Aunt Essie said you called."

"Oh, Ellen, guess what I found? After you left, I remembered another place to look. It's a book called *Bounty Claims in Alabama.* I checked and Jonas Stockman is there."

"Oooh! What does it say?"

"Jonas received land in Alabama because he fought in the Revolutionary War. He was sixty-four when he received a bounty land warrant. The record shows he served in the war from beginning to end, that's 1775 'til 1783, but he fought in South Carolina. He was married to Ruth Anne Jackson, had three sons, and he was a lawyer."

"Wow. I can't thank you enough, Miss Brenda. I'll come by the library the next time I'm in town. I want to see this with my own eyes. I'm over the moon about what we've found, Miss Brenda!"

"Well, Ellen, it's pretty exciting for me, too. See you soon."

We hang up. A lawyer. My Jonas was a lawyer. I can hardly

wait to tell Aunt Zia.

I do just that over supper. Of course, Zia is fascinated. She's so animated when she's talking about Jonas. I love to just sit back and watch her. She's come such a long way in just a few weeks. I'll never forget going to Cuba and bringing back a very different Zia, but I'm so happy to have the old Zia back.

Aunt Zia has slowly started working again, not for CBS but on her own. She's talked to me about her idea for a documentary on Cuba. She wants to do the research before approaching anyone about production. When she lived in Cuba, she heard that the former ambassador to Cuba, Arthur Gardner, was quoted as saying the U.S. State Department wanted to replace Batista with Castro. Considering the way things turned out, Aunt Zia thinks this is extremely newsworthy. I do, too.

The talk turns to my project at the plantation house. Zia and Essie think I've bitten off more than I can chew, but I don't think so. I tell them about my plan to clear the attic. I'm eager to get started and tell them, "Well, I know that you two aren't ready for bed, but I am. Gotta be at the plantation house by 8:30 in the morning. Love you, and see you tomorrow."

The next morning, I am walking up the steps of the plantation house when I see that Jack and Tom Walker have beaten me there.

"Morning, Mr. Jack and Mr. Tom. Are you the lucky ones who get to help me clean the attic?" They both grin.

"Don't know about lucky, Miss Ellen. But yes ma'am. Mr. Callander says we gotta help you," Mr. Jack says.

"Aw, Jack, you know we'd rather be helping Miss Ellen than working in the field today," Mr. Tom added.

"Well, come look at what we're doing. You may change your mind," I offer. "Can we back up Granddaddy's truck to the back porch before we go upstairs? The keys are in it. We'll start loading the truck right away. We're taking everything to that empty cotton house across the road."

Ellen and Jack wait while Tom moves the truck. Tom carefully backs up right to the porch. He turns off the engine, gets out of the truck, and lifts down the tailgate.

"We're ready, Miss Ellen," Tom says.

They walk up the wooden steps to the attic, and I watch their jaws drop. "Still want to be here instead of the field?" They don't answer. "Let's start with all these crates of *National Geographic*. The Christmas trees will be next. If ya'll don't mind, I'm gonna take the tinsel off this tree before I help you with the magazines."

I turn to the tree. It's totally covered with old tinsel, so it's hard to see what's beneath at first. I grab handfuls of the tinsel and throw them in an empty cotton basket sitting by the tree. As I remove the tinsel, I find the most amazing Christmas tree ornaments. They're made of porcelain. Little men, about five inches tall, and they are fully dressed in trousers, coats with long tails, and wool top hats. Each little man's clothes are different. I immediately fall in love with them. I envision Luke and I hanging these on our first Christmas tree. These are mine. I go downstairs to the kitchen and come back with dish towels. I wrap the men carefully and place them under the rafters.

The ornaments trigger a memory of Christmas shopping in Mobile. Mother, Daddy, and I used to go into Mobile during the first week of December to shop. The large department stores had huge, plate-glass windows, and inside each window was a Christmas scene. I loved the window with the miniature train chugging through a tiny village, decorated for Christmas. I also loved one window with a tree that was completely covered with white lights and small, porcelain Victorian ladies. The little men I just discovered remind me of that tree.

I finish removing the old tinsel and turn to the *National Geographic* magazines. I find I can carry twelve at a time, so I join Jack and Tom in the parade up and down the stairs to the back porch. Another thirty minutes and all the magazines, plus their wooden crates, are loaded into the back of the truck. I head back upstairs while Jack and Tom go to the cotton house to unload the first delivery.

Christmas trees are next. There are six of them, all standing in their tree stands, just waiting to be decorated. The tree flocked with a fluffy white spray that's supposed to be snow seems to be in the worst shape, but the one that I really dislike is the aluminum tree. I remember this one. It was in the front parlor and was decorated with blue glass ornaments. Nothing else, just blue glass ornaments. Tacky indeed.

Some of my favorite Christmas memories are going into the woods to locate the perfect tree, cut it down, and bring it home for decorating. When did people decide that these faux trees looked better? We still go to the woods every Christmas for our tree.

Jack and Tom come back with the truck, and they load the trees while I pick out what's next. The vinyl records, the dress dummy, the old patterns, and the suitcases will make up a full load. I start dragging these to the top of the stairs and take a moment to look around. It looks better. It really looks better. I see end tables I hadn't seen before, dressers and beds that I hadn't noticed, and at last, I get a clearer look at the other furniture. Some of it looks amazing. I'm totally snowed with this job.

I hear my grandfather, "Ellen, Jack and Tom are back. Come get a pimiento cheese sandwich and some iced tea before you get back to work." That really sounds good. I didn't realize I was hungry until I heard the words "pimiento cheese". Grandfather brings these up from the Callendar Store.

Jack, Tom, Grandfather, and I sit to eat lunch. Grandfather

says, "Ellen, Jack tells me you're a slave driver. Any truth to that?"

"Not a word, Granddaddy. I'm the one doing all the work."

Jack and Tom grin. We dig into the sandwiches. Dead silence. Boy, do we love pimiento cheese sandwiches made with gummy white bread.

"It's gonna take about five trips to the cotton house to get most of the furniture out of the attic. What say we do that after you take the load at the top of the steps, then we call it a day."

"Fine with us, Miss Ellen," Tom says. "It'll be dark by then, anyway."

While Jack and Tom load everything at the top of the stairs, I start looking through the furniture. It'll help if I can move most of it to one spot in the attic, at least the little pieces. I pick up a small chest and notice a paper label stuck to the back. I put the chest down for a closer look at the label. It's Duncan Phyfe. Even I know Duncan Phyfe produced expensive, well-made furniture. Someday I'm gonna have a home of my own. I think a Duncan Phyfe chest will fit right in, so I move the chest over under the rafters with my Christmas ornaments. I start moving the chairs. At the back of the attic, I find four ladder-back chairs and I immediately fall in love with them. I turn one of the chairs over—the Ethan Allen company stamp is on the bottom. So, Luke and I have kitchen chairs. Cool.

Jack, Tom, and I continue loading the truck and taking furniture to the cotton house 'til it starts getting dark. Time to call it quits. The men agree to meet me back at the plantation house at 8:30 a.m.

The next morning over breakfast I tell Essie all about the Christmas ornaments and the Duncan Phyfe chest. "And Essie,

Luke
Plans
Dreams

I found four Ethan Allen chairs. I'm saving those, too. I mean, Luke and I are going to need furniture."

Essie says, "It's like that, is it?"

"I think so, Essie. I love him, and I told him so at the wedding."

"You talked about marriage?"

"No, Essie, but I imagine we'll get around to it. Do ya think anyone would care if I ask Luke to come for the Fourth of July?"

"No, I don't. Your Dad and Amanda have been around him several times and seem to like him. I know Zia does. She invited him to the wedding."

"OK. I'm gonna call him today. Now I've got to get up and get over to the plantation house."

Just like yesterday, Jack and Tom are waiting for me on the front porch of the house.

"Mornin' guys. Back for more torture?"

"Aw, Miss Ellen, it wasn't so bad."

"I think we can get everything except the trunks today. Then you two will be finished."

Tom says, "Let's get started then."

The three of us walk up the wooden steps to the attic. At the top of the steps, I stop and look around. Wow! What a difference. There's some furniture we didn't get yesterday, a few more lamps, and tons of vinyl records. We work for hours and get everything to the cotton house.

"Well, that's it for you two. Thank you so much, guys. I could never have done this without you."

"Aw, Ellen, just tell Mr. Callander to give us a raise," says Tom with a huge grin.

"Will do, Tom. Bye guys, and thank you again."

I remember we need to tell the sharecroppers about the cotton house. "Hey, Tom, can you and Jack tell everyone that I'll open the cotton house at 7:00 p.m. tonight? It's first come, first serve." I hope most of the stuff we hauled over can be used by the families.

I want to sweep and mop the attic floor before lunch, so I go back to the house, get my supplies, and head upstairs. I start sweeping. Ugh! I don't think this floor has ever been swept. I finally finish the floor, and hear, "Ellen, it's turkey sandwiches today, and I've got some lemon icebox pie."

"Thanks, Granddaddy. I'll be right there."

Granddaddy and I sit in comfortable silence chewing our turkey sandwiches. When we finish, I tell him all we've accomplished and let him know I'm opening the cotton house to the sharecroppers and their families tonight.

"Child, you're a whiz. I should have put you in charge of the attic years ago."

"Don't forget the trunks. It'll take weeks to go through them. And you're right, that's a project for next summer or maybe right after Christmas when it's not so dang hot up in the attic."

"Whatever you want to do, child."

"Think I'll go back up to the attic and see what I'm dealing with. Don't know how many trunks are up there." I give him a kiss on the forehead. "Talk to ya later, Granddaddy."

Back in the attic, I count eleven trunks. No wait, there are twelve. One is sitting all alone at the very back of the attic by the attic windows.

I'll just take a peek at that one trunk, and I'll leave.

This trunk seems older than the others and more primitive somehow. It has a flat top like some of the other trunks. It's covered with some kind of hide with iron locks and handles. The tongue of the trunk lock is hanging loose. I grab it and lift the lid of the trunk.

The first thing I notice is the inside of the lid—it's lined with a dull, gray paper as is the tray of the trunk. Inside the trunk tray, I see what looks like journals made of leather and tied with a leather thong. I see old letters and newspaper articles. That's when I see the name on the letters: *Jonas Stockman.* I sit on the floor with a plop. My mouth is so dry I think my tongue could stick to the roof of my mouth. I feel a little light-headed.

I reach into the trunk and bring out one of the journals. It's so old. I hear pages crackle as I open the journal to the first page. *Jonas Stockman, 1775 – 1783* is written on the first page. That's during the Revolutionary War. I carefully turn to the middle of the journal and read:

October 1780. Heavy fighting at King's Mountain. We took them by surprise. Bastards surrendered after Ferguson shot. Retreated in a hurry because of Cornwallis. Victory for us.

Further on in the journal I read these words:

20 November 1780. Blackstock's Farm. Our men holed up in the outbuildings on the farm. The one I was in smelled like a smokehouse. We had the best position, on high

ground. We just waited until Tarleton's troops attacked,
and we beat the tar out of them. Sumter is some more soldier.

I carefully close Jonas' journal and place it back in the tray. I know who I've got to tell first. Aunt Zia. Granddaddy is nowhere around when I come downstairs so I go out the front door and head home. I'm pretty sure where I'll find Zia. She works on a little round table on the back porch. She always wants to be outside.

I don't want to frighten her, so I yell as I go through the house, "Aunt Zia, you'd better be sitting down."

Sure enough, she's on the porch. She is so beautiful with her smooth, milky skin and long hair pinned in a twist at the back of her head with a wooden hair fork. She's leaning over her work but looks up when I walk on the porch.

"You'll never guess, Aunt Zia. If you had a million years, you'd never guess."

Zia says, "What are you talking about, child?"

"I found Jonas! I found Jonas Stockman."

"You mean Miss Brenda at the library found him?"

"No, I did. I really did."

I explain to Aunt Zia about all the trunks in the attic and about the one standing alone that I opened. I tell her about the articles, letters, and journals. "Aunt Zia, I think we need to read them together."

"Oh, Ellen. I can hardly believe it. All those stories that we made up about Jonas, and he was up in the attic the entire time!"

"I know, Aunt Zia. Can you make a day of it tomorrow? We'll start early in the morning and read all day."

"Yes, that way I can finish part of the research I'm doing."

"Good, and I need to talk to Luke, plus get the cotton house organized for tonight."

"Give Luke my love."

"I will. I'm asking him to come for the Fourth of July."

"Perfect. See you at supper, dear."

I walk into the hall and sit down by the phone. I've got little flutters in my stomach. I dial the long-distance operator and ask for Luke's number.

I hear a sleepy-sounding Luke answer, "Hello."

"Wake up, you lazy bum. What are you doing sleeping in the afternoon?"

"Well, hi darling. No on the lazy bum. I was up all night covering a story about a campus murder."

"Oh goodness. I'm so sorry. Want me to call later?"

"Silly girl, of course not."

"Well, I want to hear all about the murder, but I called to see if you can come to Callander for the Fourth."

"I heard all about your grandfather's famous barbecue at the wedding. Sure, I'll be there."

"You're coming for the barbecue then?"

"Fishing, aren't ya? Naw, darling, I'm coming to see you. I'm dying here without you."

Ignoring that comment, I say, "Why don't ya get here the day before?"

"I can do that, Cotton."

I wait for a second then say, "You know I love you to *love* distraction?"

"I love you to distraction, too. We have a lot to talk about, Ellen."

"Yes, we do. It'll be great to be alone and talk about us. We haven't had time to do that. I'll take you to Jonas' grave. We'll be alone there."

"We're gonna make love on a grave?"

"Luke! No, it's just my special place on the plantation."

"By the way, what about this murder?"

"Forever the reporter, right Cotton?"

Luke starts to tell me about the murder on campus. By the time I hang up the phone, Essie sticks her head in the door and says, "Suppertime."

Over dinner, I fill Essie in on all the other things I found in the attic but don't mention Jonas. I tell Zia and Essie about my conversation with Luke. "He's coming on the third. That's the end of next week. Should I fix up a room for him at the plantation house? Not enough room here."

"I'll do that, child. Don't worry about that," Essie offers.

"Thank you, Essie. Now, I've got to get down to the cotton house."

The cotton house stands near the store, and I wave to some of the sharecroppers who are standing around outside. I walk up to the cotton house and open one of the large, wooden double doors. It's musty and airless inside. I go back and open the other door to let the sunshine stream into the house.

Jack and Tom have done an unreal job. Instead of throwing everything in the cotton house, they grouped everything. All the furniture is at the back of the house, and all the lamps are together. Everything we took out of the attic is grouped that way.

There's not much for me to do. I go up to the plantation house and get a broom. I can sweep out the center of the house and try to get some of the cobwebs down. By the time I finish, I hear the sharecroppers coming, and I hear Granddaddy bragging on the job I've done.

I stick my head outside the cotton house and say, "Hello, everybody. Thank you for coming. We've got furniture, lamps, Christmas trees—come on in. Whatever you don't take is going back to Granddaddy's attic."

"Over my dead body," says Granddaddy.

Everyone mills around and by nine o'clock only the *National Geographic* magazines are left. Even the aluminum tree is gone. Everyone goes home with their loot, and Granddaddy and I are left alone.

"Ellen, you amaze me, child. Here's seventy-five dollars, you earned it. Don't forget those trunks are still waiting."

I smile at Granddaddy. I'm not ready to tell him about the Jonas trunk until I've shown it to Aunt Zia. We lock arms and walk out of the cotton house.

"Granddaddy, I'm coming back to the attic in the morning."

"No problem, child. I won't be around. I've got to be in Marshall by eight. The mayor and I are gonna chew the fat about some things."

Good. I don't have to explain Aunt Zia and me in the attic.

"I love you, Granddaddy." I give him a tight hug.

"I love you, too. Sleep tight tonight."

To my surprise, I really do sleep tight. When I wake up, it takes a minute to get my bearings. Then I remember that Aunt Zia and I are gonna find Jonas today! You know that feeling ya get on Christmas morning? It's like that. Exactly like that. I throw on my pedal pushers and a blouse and hurry downstairs. Essie and Aunt Zia are already downstairs drinking coffee. I grin at Aunt Zia.

"I'm off to Marshall. Gotta start getting my house ready to move back in," Essie announces.

"Essie, you know we'll help with that."

"I know, Ellen. I know, but I've gotta take a look and see what needs to be done before I get you to help me."

"See you for lunch?" I ask.

"Nope. I'm gonna have lunch with Eleanor."

"Have a good day." I hug Essie.

"When times are good, be happy. Ecclesiastes 7:14."

After Essie walks out the back door, I turn to Zia and squeal, "I can't eat a bite. I'd choke. Let's go, Aunt Zia. Come on, let's go."

"Do I have time to get dressed?"

"Only if you hurry." I smile and stick out my tongue.

Today we drive up to the plantation house. I explain to Aunt Zia about Granddaddy being in Marshall. I lead as we walk in the house, and I remember we're gonna need chairs. We can't sit on that floor all day.

"Aunt Zia, will you hold the attic door? I need to get a couple of these chairs up to the attic."

"Sure."

I grab a couple of the ladder-back chairs from the kitchen and bang my way up the attic stairs with them. Zia follows and takes in the attic.

"It's the one back by the windows," I say.

I drag the chairs over to the trunk, open the trunk lid, and sit down. Aunt Zia places her hands on both ends of the tray and lifts it. I didn't look under the tray yesterday. There's some type of clothing in the trunk, and a large Bible on top. Zia sets the tray on the floor. I lay the Bible on the floor beside the tray and lift the top piece of clothing. Despite the moth holes, it looks pretty good. It's a white linen affair—looks like it would fall near the knee, but I don't know how tall Jonas was. It has a cape that runs beneath the collar, and I guess it tied at the waist with a sash because there's one attached.

"This is strange. . ."

"Not so strange, Ellen. The men couldn't afford uniforms. Many of them wore these hunting frocks."

The next garment is a waistcoat. Even I know that. It's nutmeg-colored with buttons from top to bottom. No sleeves, of course. There are pants under the waistcoat, but I leave them where they are because a haversack catches my eye. Jonas would have carried his war rations and supplies in this coarsely woven bag slung over his shoulder. The stains on the haversack look like old blood and who knows what. Not a very romantic ensemble. *Thought all the soldiers dressed like George Washington? Guess not.*

Zia picks up the Bible. She lifts up a group of pages in the middle of the Bible and lets them fall open one by one. She stops. The Bible opens to a page with cursive handwriting on it. The word, *Register*, is printed at the top of the page in an ornate script. There are scrolls within scrolls, so it's hard to make it out. Scrolls from the word Register run down both sides of the page. Underneath the word Register, the word <u>*Births*</u> is written. These births are written in cursive:

James Horace Stockman
Born October 9, 1753
Craven County, South Carolina

Ruth Anne Jackson
Born June 25, 1750
Craven County, South Carolina

John William Stockman
Born June 11, 1772
Craven County, South Carolina

Horace Lee Stockman
Born May 22, 1773
Craven County, South Carolina

Jeffery Douglas Stockman
Born June 1, 1775
Craven County, South Carolina

"Look, Aunt Zia. Three sons. Wonder why the book Miss Brenda found showed him living alone?"

Zia turns the page. She's very still as she reads. "This is why, Ellen." She hands the Bible to me.

The top of the next page is a duplicate of the previous page except instead of the word Births, the word Deaths is written. It shows the following:

Horace Lee Stockman
August 11, 1773

Jeffery Douglas Stockman
July 4, 1776

John William Stockman
March 27, 1814

Ruth Anne Jackson
April 2, 1819

"Aunt Zia, his first two children died when they were so small. Wonder what happened?"

"Who knows? There were so many diseases. They could have gotten malaria or yellow fever from mosquito bites."

"How sad for Jonas. And Ruth. I can't imagine being a parent and losing your children."

"And Jonas and Ruth lost all of them."

I put the uniform back in the trunk. I fold it very carefully because Jonas wore it. At least I think he wore it. Zia adds the Bible to the top and lifts the tray back into place.

"What do you want to look at next, Ellen?"

"Well, we know a little about his family. I want to know how he landed in Alabama. How 'bout this journal? It's dated 1813—1814."

"Sure."

11 June 1813. John turns forty-one today. Hate to think that he spends his birthday fighting Indians. One thing, he sure loves Alabama. Miss him.

"Ah," Zia says. "John is fighting in the Alabama territory."

1 March 1814. Got letter from John William. Fighting with Andrew Jackson. Talk in Alabama territory about soldiers applying for a warrant to get a land patent. Includes Revolutionary War soldiers. Wants me to apply when can.

I gasp when I see the next entry.

10 April 1814. Got letter today from General Jackson. John William died in the Battle of Horseshoe Bend on 27 March 1814. Our last child. Give me strength to tell Ruth.

I look through the journal. There are no more entries.

"I think our Jonas had a very sad life," Zia sighs.

"I know. And we still don't know why he was living alone in Alabama. That's in the 1820 Census. That seems the saddest thing to me, for him to be all alone."

"This may have the answer. It's a journal dated 1817–1819."

9 October 1817. I turn 64 today. Ruth and I leave South Carolina today. Leave from Charleston. Get on a steamer that will take us to Mobile. Have land patent for land in town of Marshall's Ridge.

"OK, Aunt Zia. This is how he gets to Alabama." I point to the next entry.

18 October 1817. Landed in Mobile. Steamers all lined up at dockyards. Cobblestone street at the dock stacked with lumber and sacks of cotton. Much like Charleston but smaller. People different. Besides whites, see large numbers of negroes and Indians. Will buy wagon to get to Marshall's Ridge.

I turn through some pages and say, "Look at this, Aunt Zia."

Jonas
Truth &
Honor

15 November 1817. Set up law practice in Holman's store. Moved my desk to back of store and settled in between barrels of potatoes and bolts of cloth. My old "Truth and Honor" plaque is on my desk. Ready for business!

16 November 1817. Got a client today. Lucy Grimes hired

me to bring charges against Sam Grubb for shooting her
mule. Seems cut and dried.

I flip through the pages and stop at the entry for March 25.
I read:

25 March 1819. Worried about Ruth. Has fever and
complains of sore throat. Bright red spots on chest.

The next to last entry reads:

2 April 1819. I lost my Ruth today. Scarlett Fever.
Putting her remains on a ship back to Craven County for
burial.

The last entry was probably anticlimactic for Jonas, but it is
very important for Alabama. I read aloud: "*14 December 1819.*
Alabama becomes a state today."

"That's a lot of sadness for one morning. Let's go get lunch."

"Suits me," I answer. "Wanna get sandwiches from the store
and eat on the front porch?"

"Sure."

Aunt Zia and I walk across the road to the commissary or
store. Since it's noon, there's a bunch of sharecroppers hanging
out on the porch.

"Mornin' Ellen," says Jo Jo's Dad. "Hear you are gonna have
Jo Jo to dinner."

"That's right, Mr. Reed. Hope we can do that tomorrow
night. I'll talk to Jo Jo this afternoon."

Aunt Zia and I walk into the store. Clothes are on the left side of the store, and food is on the right. Drink cases with flat tops and attached bottle openers are on the right side of the store. One of my favorite things to do is to lift one of the heavy lids and stick my head inside. Sure cools you off.

Today, I resist the temptation and walk down to the counter running from the drink cases to the back wall. Sandwiches wrapped in heavy waxed paper are scattered on top of the counter. Today there's turkey, pimiento and cheese, and roast beef.

Wally runs the store on most days, and today he's standing behind the counter. I pick up a turkey sandwich and say, "Hey, Wally. You busy today?"

"Well, you can see, Miss Ellen. There's a regular stampede in here to buy my sandwiches."

I look around. There's no one in the store except Zia and I. "Aw, Wally. They don't know what they're missing."

The wooden counters that the sandwiches are on have glass fronts; my mouth waters as I see Stage Planks, Sugar Babies, and Mars Bars inside.

"Wally, I've gotta have one of those Mars Bars. I'll take one for Aunt Zia, too."

"They'll rot your teeth, Miss Ellen."

"I know, Wally, but aren't they great?"

Aunt Zia and I say goodbye to Wally. We make our way across the road to the plantation house and each take a seat in a large rocker. For a while, we just rock and eat.

I'm thinking again about Aunt Zia and all she went through in Cuba. I know she talks to Julio, but I don't know about David.

"Aunt Zia, have you heard from Uncle David yet?"

Her brow furrows. She answers, "No. It's been a month now, and I haven't heard a thing. I pray that Castro didn't punish him because I'm gone."

"I'll help you pray, Aunt Zia." I don't know what else to say.

We rock for a while, and Aunt Zia suggests that we get back to the journals. When we get back upstairs to the trunk, Aunt Zia counts the journals. There's six more with the last one covering the years 1828 and 1829. We know Jonas died in 1829, so we save that journal for last.

We each take a couple of journals and look through them. Almost all the entries deal with Jonas' court cases. Sometimes he mentions life in Marshall's Ridge. In 1827, the town was incorporated and officially became Marshall. They dropped the Ridge.

By four o'clock, we're bleary-eyed and agree to quit. We make a plan to look at the newspaper articles tomorrow before we look at the last journal. We carefully place everything back in the trunk, say goodbye to Jonas, and head home for the night.

Essie is there when we get home.

"Aunt Essie, before I forget—can Jo Jo eat dinner with us tomorrow night?"

"Sure, Ellen. We're having County Captain."

"Jo Jo loves your Country Captain. I'll let him know. Eat at six o'clock?"

"Sure."

That night, over dinner, Aunt Zia and I tell Essie about finding Jonas. Essie is stunned. We take turns telling her about his children, their moving to Marshall, and the death of his wife. Silence.

Finally, Essie says, "We must go through many hardships to enter the kingdom of God. Acts 14:22."

The next morning, Aunt Zia and I are back at Callander by 8:30 a.m. Grandfather shouts as we walk into the hall, "That you, Jack?"

"It's me Granddaddy. Aunt Zia is with me."

"Well, come in the kitchen. What's going on?"

Zia and I walk in to find Granddaddy sitting at the kitchen table drinking coffee. I guess it's time to tell him about Jonas.

"Well, Granddaddy, we have some news. I found a trunk in the attic that's filled with Jonas Stockman's things. Zia and I have been going through journals, and this morning we're going through some newspaper articles."

"That's wonderful, Ellen. I know Jonas has always been special to you. I can't wait to hear his story, but this morning I've got to get to Marshall by nine o'clock. I've got a meeting with the insurance folks."

I get up and go kiss him on the forehead. "Have a good day, Granddaddy. We're going up to the attic now."

"Bye, child. We'll talk later."

Aunt Zia and I head up the stairs, open the trunk, and pull out the newspaper articles.

"Let's put them in chronological order before we read them."

"Great plan," I say. We quickly put them in order, and I pick up the top article.

"This one is about a murder in Marshall."

17 April, 1828. Dolly Sullivan was found murdered in Miss Sarah Owen's millinery shop yesterday. Miss Sarah opened the shop at nine o'clock and found Dolly's body on the floor of the shop. Dolly appears to have been strangled. She worked for Miss Sarah for eight years. She stitched ribbons and flowers on the hats Miss Sarah created. Dolly was in her early twenties and was mute. Sheriff Earl has indicated that he will start interviewing shop owners today.

The murder of Dolly Sullivan appears to be tied to the robbery of Miss Sarah's Millinery. Sheriff Earl states that the cash register drawer was open, and all the money was taken. Miss Sarah states there was around one hundred dollars in the drawer. Dolly was employed by Miss Sarah for eight years. Sheriff Earl continues to interview shop owners on Main Street.

"This is strange, Aunt Zia. Wonder what it has to do with Jonas?"

"I don't know, but there's a connection or these articles would not be in Jonas' trunk. And furthermore, why is Jonas' trunk here in the attic? We've been so excited about finding Jonas that we haven't asked this question."

Tom George is accused of the murder of Dolly Sullivan. George was arrested yesterday following an accusation by the wife of Mayor Hudson, Lorraine Hudson. Mrs. Hudson told Sheriff Earl that she saw Tom George enter Miss Sarah's Millinery on the evening of April 16th. Dolly Sullivan was found murdered the morning of April 17th by Miss Sarah. Sullivan appears to have been strangled.

20 April 1928. Tom George guilty? Sheriff Earl told the Marshall Times-
Standard that George swears he was in Mobile on April 16, 1828. George
said he had gone to Mobile to meet the steamer and pick up flour,
sugar, and tea for Mr. Holman at the general store. Mayor Hudson's wife,
Lorraine, swears she saw Tom George entering the millinery the night of
April 16. George is a Catawba Indian who fought in the Revolutionary
War and came to Marshall with Mr. Holman when he moved here in 1815.

"Ellen, Tom George doesn't have a prayer. Creek Indians
raided and killed settlers living away from the towns in Alabama.
I've read most white settlers were afraid of the Indians, all of
them, and they probably *tolerated* Tom George because of Mr.
Holman."

"You're right about Tom George's chances. Who would
believe him over the mayor's wife?"

"There are only a few more articles. Let's finish these and go
back to Jonas' journal."

I look at the article that Zia hands me. It's dated 23 April
1828:

Emotions are high over the murder of Dolly Sullivan. On the night of
April 22, a crowd of men gathered at the jail and demanded Sheriff Earl
hand over Tom George to them. The men planned to take George out of
town and kill him. Bill Wilson, leader of the group, promised to strangle
George just like George had strangled Dolly. Sheriff Earl convinced the
group to return to their homes. A preliminary hearing begins tomorrow in
front of Judge Collins.

"Aunt Zia, I vote for going back to the journal now. We
need to find out how this involved Jonas."

"I agree but it's almost lunch time. Wanna take a break?"

"Yes, but I don't want a sandwich from the store. I think I'll run into town for a burger. Wanna come?"

"No, I think I'll walk home and eat leftovers. Would you like to meet back here at one o'clock?"

"That sounds good. I may run by and fill Miss Brenda in on what we've found. By the way, we need to stop at four o'clock. I want to help Aunt Essie get ready for dinner with Jo Jo."

I walk back home with Zia and get the car. On the way into Marshall, I clear my mind by turning on WVBK, a radio station out of Mobile. They are playing Bobby Vee's Take Good Care of My Baby. I think of Luke.

I grab a burger at the local drive-in then run by the library. Miss Brenda is eating lunch in a back room. I eat my burger with her. It's nice to eat lunch surrounded by old books. I tell her all we've learned about Jonas.

"Ellen, how fortuitous you found the trunk. Like you, I want to know why it's in your grandfather's attic. Please come back soon and update me."

I say goodbye to Miss Brenda and turn to leave. "Ellen, wait a minute—I almost forgot. Mrs. Maben left this for you." Miss Brenda hands me a pale blue envelope smelling of lavender. "She didn't explain. Just said please give it to you when I see you."

I thank Miss Brenda, take the envelope, and head back to Callander. I know where I'll open it—Jonas Stockman's grave but, as curious as I am, that will have to wait. As I enter the plantation house, I hear sounds from the attic. Aunt Zia has beaten me back to Jonas.

"Ellen, here is the journal dated 1828-1829. Would you like

me to start at the beginning?"

"We can go back to that later. Let's start in April of 1828."

"Good idea." I search through the journal until the entry for April 17 catches my eye. I read:

17 April 1828. In Mobile for trial of Jacob Hobb. Expect trial to last at least a week. <u>Ran into Tom George during trial recess.</u> We walked down to the wharf and ate a bite together sitting and dangling our feet over the bay. He was picking up goods for Holman's store and will head back to Marshall tomorrow. Wondered where he stays since Indians aren't allowed in the hotels. Told me he stayed with friends in a settlement right outside town and will head home tomorrow.

"Aunt Zia, <u>Tom George was innocent. Jonas saw him in Mobile. Let me keep looking.</u>"

The next pages are about the Jacob Hobb trial until I get to the entries marked April 24 and April 25.

Truth

24 April 1828. Got back to town last night. Hear that the town is ready to hang Tom George for murder of Dolly Stockman. Dolly was murdered April 17. Mayor Hudson's wife told Sheriff Earl that she saw Tom George in the store the night before. That can't be. I saw Tom in Mobile and that's a day's ride from Marshall. Gotta set this straight.

25 April 1828. Went to see Judge Collins before the hearing started. Told him I was with Tom George in Mobile and that I needed to testify. He told me I'd be

sorry if I testified. Mayor Hudson could do me harm. Nobody goes against the mayor. Judge Collins thinks I'll be ruined if I tell the truth.

25 April 1828. Judge Collins let me testify after hearing started. Could hear a pin drop in court when I finished. Mayor gave me dirty looks. Wife wouldn't look at me. Did she lie? Did she see someone who looked like Tom? I had to tell the truth. "Truth and Honor."

Truth + Honor

Aunt Zia sighed. "Well, Ellen. Jonas lived by his code. I admire him for that. What's next?"

I read the next entry:

26 April 1828. Got to Holman's store to work. Front of store covered with words, "Indian Lover" written in red paint. Mr. Holman went to hearing this morning. Came back to store late morning with Tom George. Judge ruled no evidence to hold Tom. Tom thanked me for testifying. He says that his God, He-Who-Never-Dies, sent me to testify.

"OK, Aunt Zia. I'm looking through this journal and don't see another entry until June. This one is dated 25 June."

25 June 1828. Things are bad. Haven't had a case since the Hobbs's case in April. People resent me for testifying. Am sure the mayor is stirring them up. Bad for Holman's store, too. Mr. Holman and Tom plan to move back to South Carolina. Catawbas have secured reservation on their original land because they fought in the Revolutionary War. South Carolina paid them, too. For their service in the War. Tom will go to the reservation.

"Aunt Zia, that's it for the journal. There are some newspaper articles that we haven't read, right?"

"Yes, there's a couple. Here."

I look at the article. "This one's an obituary—for Jonas." I read aloud: "*Jonas H. Stockman died unexpectedly in Marshall, Alabama, on 9 May 1829 at the age of seventy-five. He is preceded in death by wife, Ruth Anne Jackson, and his sons, Horace Lee, Jeffery Douglas, and John William Stockman. Jonas was born on 9 October 1753 in Craven County, South Carolina. He received a law degree from the College of William and Mary and practiced law in Marshall for eleven years. His funeral is scheduled for 11 May at four o'clock at Marshall Methodist Church.*"

I look at Aunt Zia. Her head is bent over the last article. She looks up at me and reads: "*Thomas Henry Callander buried Jonas H. Stockman on Callander land on the afternoon of 11 May after funeral rites were observed for the aforementioned at Marshall Methodist Church. Callander was quoted as saying that Jonas Stockman was a man of honor who told the truth and was shunned for it. Thomas Henry Callander further states Jonas deserved a place to rest on the land of a man who respected him.*"

"My great, great grandfather must have taken his belongings and stored them in the attic at Callander," I say.

"That makes sense, Ellen. That's probably what happened." Some minutes pass before Zia says, "It's almost four o'clock; we'd better go home to help Essie."

I just sit. Trying to take in all about Jonas. I finally get up, but, instead of following Aunt Zia home, I walk to Jonas' grave. I settle down on the grassy earth by the grave and open the blue envelope smelling of lavender. My hands tremble as I remove the thin, blue sheets of stationary. I read:

Dear Ellen,

I know you'll be shocked to hear from me. I've felt a strong need to talk with you, even if it's by letter. I think you're having a hard time, and maybe I can help in some small way.

Of course, John didn't kill Ann Carson. First, let me tell you that I'm aware that your mother could have saved John. I know that you are aware of this as well. Second, let me tell you that I have forgiven your mother. My faith teaches me to forgive, and I've learned over the years that it is the right thing to do.

I think that you are feeling very ashamed of your mother's actions. I encourage you to forgive as well. Remember the beautiful lady who was a good mother to you.

God bless,

Deborah Maben

I feel the knot forming in my chest, and the tears begin to roll down my face. This remarkable woman is trying to make me feel better about the deaths of her husband and my mother. I lower my face to the dry, brittle grass and cry. Finally, I feel limp. I silently thank Mrs. Maben, knowing the courage it took for her to write this letter.

When I get home, I smell chicken frying. Nobody can fry chicken like Aunt Essie. When the chicken is fried, she'll add onions, peppers, garlic, and tomatoes. She'll add rice, raisins, and almonds. Jo Jo is in for a real treat.

Speaking of Jo Jo, he'll be here in an hour. After hugging Essie, I head upstairs to shower off the smell of the attic at Callander. If Aunt Essie notices my swollen face, she says nothing.

Jo Jo knocks on the door promptly at six o'clock. Aunt Zia answers the door and asks Jo Jo to come in. He brought three pearly-pink roses with him—one for Zia, one for Essie, and one for me. He hands me a rose as I come down the stairs.

"Jo Jo, you are a true gentleman."

Aunt Essie sticks her head out of the kitchen door and says, "Hello Jo Jo. Ya'll come on in the kitchen. We're gonna eat in here."

"Here's a rose for you, Miss Essie. And I hear we're having Country Captain."

"That's right, Jo Jo. Come on in, and let's start dinner."

Over dinner, Aunt Zia and I tell Aunt Essie and Jo Jo all about Jonas.

"Ellen, I know how attached you've been to the idea of Jonas and how often you go to his grave. In all the stories you've made up about him, did you ever come close to his true story?"

"No, Jo-Jo, I never came anywhere near his real story."

"Ellen, now that you've found Jonas, think about how this ties in with Luella's predictions for you. Didn't she predict that you'd find the soldier?"

"You're right, Aunt Zia." I speak the three predictions aloud, "She will be an advocate for the beauty; She will find the soldier; She will foil a dictator."

"I guess I'm through with Luella's predictions—and I'm only twenty-one."

"Ellen, don't you know about Luella? Her predictions are for a lifetime," Jo-Jo says. "You may repeat these predictions during your life."

"That's right, Ellen. That's what everybody says. I have a neighbor in town whose son is in his forties and he has protected a president twice in his life so far," Aunt Zia says. "Look at it this way, Ellen. Luella's predictions for you are so powerful. They indicate you are a strong person who will make a difference." She smiles and adds, "*Truth and Honor*."

We talk about Jo Jo's first duty station at Tripoli, about Aunt Essie moving back to town, and about Aunt Zia's documentary on Cuba. It's so comfortable, all the conversations swirling around the table. I think about Luke. He comes to Callander tomorrow. Dad and Amanda should be home tomorrow, too. For right now, in this moment, life is wonderful at Callander but I look forward to the days ahead at college.

Fall semester starts in a few days. I visit the attic at the plantation house before I leave and marvel at how clean and empty it is. There are still rows of trunks left to go through. I lift the lid of the trunk that contains all of Jonas' belongings, removing the tray of journals and newspaper clippings.

Holding Jonas' hunting frock close to my face, I breathe in deeply. Visualizing in my head the battles, the campfires surrounded by soldiers, and the agonies of seeing friends wounded or dying, I can almost smell the smoke from campfires. I can almost taste the iron-like tang of blood.

What a life our Jonas led, I think. As I place the waistcoat on top of the other clothes, I accidentally move the trunk with my foot. I hear something solid shift in the bottom. Puzzled, I lift out all the clothing—there in the bottom of the trunk is a triangular desk sign made of solid wood. Engraved on a brass plaque are the familiar words *Truth and Honor.* I beg Jonas' forgiveness as I remove the sign from the trunk taking it with me when I leave the attic.

Ellen's Notebook: 1960–1961

ON AIR PERFORMERS

Anchors

Anchors deliver the news on television. They work in the studio and perform with an entire crew that makes their news report happen. Anchors have the luxury of using a teleprompter, and they introduce the various reporters.

Reporters

Reporters deliver the news as well but are usually reporting from 'out in the field', accompanied by a cameraman. They have to perform with a lot of noise and activity going on around them.

Stuff to Remember if I'm Ever on Air
(besides what Luke taught me)

Enunciate. Say each word distinctly. When reading a newspaper, the reader can read and reread the story until he understands it. In television news, the viewer has one chance to get all the information.

Slow down. Back to saying each word distinctly. When you slow down, just make sure that you don't slow your pacing too much. You don't want the audience waiting for your next word. Be natural. Make sure that you know how to pronounce each word.

Practice by saying these sentences. Open your mouth wide and exaggerate each word:

> Pretty Penny planted plenty.

> Hark, hark, the lark.

> Didn't Daddy drive downtown?

> Around the rugged rock, the ragged rascal ran.

Watch your inflection, and notice which words you stress. You can change the meaning of the story by putting inflection on the wrong word.

She wore the red dress. (The dress was red, not blue.)

She wore the red dress. (She, not Donna, wore the red dress.)

She wore the red dress. (She wore a dress, not pants.)

Practice, practice, practice!

Reporters should record the entire story in the field even though B-roll will be added over the story later. The audio will sound better. Remember, ambient noise will be in story throughout for continuity.

This is a shot Lewis Henry took of Jenny Lake in Wyoming. I love this picture. Mr. Henry gave it to me for my notebook.

ETHICS

I was so upset about the story Amanda ran on the campus president. This is a reminder to check-out the "Code of Broadcasting" created in the early 1950s.

COMPOSITION RULES

Rule of Thirds

Composition Rule #1 - Use imaginary lines to divide the viewfinder of a camera into thirds horizontally and vertically. What you have looks like tic-tac-toe. Use the lines to compose drawings or shots so that the center(s) of interest falls on the lines themselves or where the lines intersect.

This visual will be more interesting than a visual where your center of interest is placed in the middle. That's dull and boring. Use the grid to compose close-ups of people and animals. Draw so the eyes of the subject are on the top line or, in other words, a third of the way down the grid. Eyes should not be in the center of the drawing. This would result in too much headroom.

Leading Looks or Nose Room

Composition Rule #2 - Lead room, also called nose room. When shooting the profile of a person, allow empty space in the direction where the person is looking. This also applies to side views of cars driving down the road, or football players running down the field; any shot that shows a side view of the subject. In the car example, more space is allowed in front of the car; the car needs room to move forward in the picture.

In television, lead room is important for interviews. The interviewee should look eyes-right or eyes-left, not directly into the camera lens. Lead room is provided so the interviewee has room to look into the frame.

Leading Lines

Composition Rule #3 - Leading lines. Occasionally, you may use natural lines in the environment to lead toward your subject. The lines may include fences, roads, pathways, or the edge of a highway. Place your subject at the end of the line, and the viewer's eye will follow the line to your subject.

Notice how the line of tulips leads to the White House.

Framing

Composition Rule #4 - Framing. You may wish to frame your subject with objects in the environment; either completely frame the subject or partially frame the subject.

When I think of framing, I think of that shot from the movie, "Gone with the Wind". Scarlet and her father are seen from behind and partially framed with that wonderful old tree filling the left side and top third of the frame.

Jeff Smith took this shot of the Scottish countryside, framed by a roughly-hewn, stone window.

A final thought on composition is background. The subject or center of interest is the most important element in the drawing. Watch for busy backgrounds that blend with your subject or detract from your subject.

About the Author

Alayne Smith is a retired broadcast journalism teacher who earned M.Ed and Ed.S degrees in Instructional Technology from the University of Georgia. She taught broadcast journalism for fifteen years in Gwinnett County, Ga., where she developed the first broadcast journalism course at the high school level. With other Gwinnett County broadcast journalism teachers, she contributed to the development of an eight-course continuum of courses in broadcast journalism and video production.

Two of Alayne's students won the 1999 Southern Regional Student Emmy Award from the National Academy of Arts and Sciences. Sixty students produced documentaries and feature stories, advancing to International Media Festivals held in New Orleans, Dallas, Houston, Indianapolis, and Denver. She served as a committee member for the International Student Media Festival, 1995-1998, and as a CNN Student Bureau Advisor, 1999 – 2001.

While working at the Broadcast and Learning Department of Gwinnett County Public Schools, Alayne designed classes, developed manuals, and co-taught the following for Gwinnett County teachers and staff: Casablanca Editing System: Advanced TST Training, Retrofit: Broadcast Studio Equipment, Getting More Out of Your Morning Newscast, Avid Edit Systems for Adobe Photoshop Users. In fall of 2011, Alayne co-presented Using Windows Movie Maker at the COMO (Georgia Council of Media Organizations) annual conference.

In 2008, Alayne developed a cluster training approach for media specialists, K-8, to maximize the use of each school's broadcast equipment. She co-taught sessions in each of the county's seventeen clusters, reaching media specialists from over ninety-six schools. Media Specialists were offered hands-on instruction to assist them with creating informative, curricula-based, attention-getting broadcasts.

Alayne is a member of the Georgia Association for Instructional Technology, Gwinnett County Retired Educators Association, Phi Kappa Phi, and the Society of Children's Book Writers and Illustrators. She currently lives in Lawrenceville, Ga., with her husband.

More YA from Saturn's Moon Press

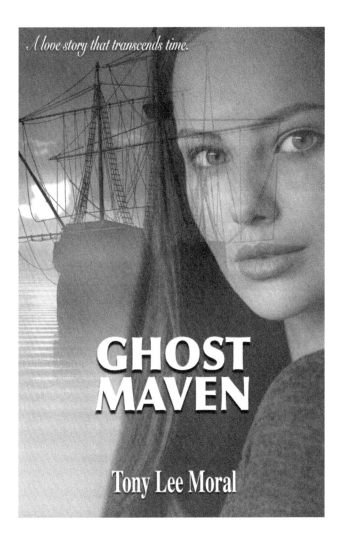

By Tony Lee Moral

Available on Amazon and most online retailers.

CPSIA information can be obtained
at www.ICGtesting.com
Printed in the USA
LVOW06s1326110817
544656LV00023B/78/P